MITIGATING CIRCUMSTANCES

MITIGATING CIRCUMSTANCES

DAWN CORRIGAN

FIVE STAR
A part of Gale, Cengage Learning

GALE
CENGAGE Learning®

Detroit • New York • San Francisco • New Haven, Conn • Waterville, Maine • London

GALE
CENGAGE Learning®

LIBRARY OF CONGRESS CATALOGING-IN-PUBLICATION DATA

Corrigan, Dawn.
    Mitigating circumstances / Dawn Corrigan. — First Edition.
        pages cm
    ISBN-13: 978-1-4328-2779-3 (hardcover)
    ISBN-10: 1-4328-2779-0 (hardcover)
    1. Kidnapping—Fiction. 2. City planners—Fiction. 3. Gulf Breeze (Fla.) —Fiction. I. Title.
PS3603.O7727M58 2014
813'.6—dc23   2013031753

First Edition. First Printing: December 2013
Find us on Facebook– https://www.facebook.com/FiveStarCengage
Visit our website– http://www.gale.cengage.com/fivestar/
Contact Five Star™ Publishing at FiveStar@cengage.com

Printed in Mexico
1 2 3 4 5 6 7 17 16 15 14 13

MITIGATING CIRCUMSTANCES

CHAPTER ONE

"Don't you come a step closer! You get off my property right now, you hear! If you don't, I'm allowed to stab ya! I read all about it in the papers."

The speaker was 56-year-old Jackie Willis, who stood on the tiny, lopsided front porch of her mobile home, wearing a mis-buttoned housecoat and fuzzy pink bedroom slippers, pointing an oversized bread knife at the spot where I stood on her overgrown lawn.

Not for the first time, it occurred to me that perhaps I should have chosen a different line of work. I'm the Junior City Planner for the City of Gulf Breeze, Florida, population 5,763. In a city the size of Gulf Breeze, the Junior Planner is often stuck doing Code Enforcement, which is what had brought me to the Willis residence this fine morning.

"I'm just here to talk to you about your yard, Ms. Willis."

"I'm not scared of you damn city people!" Jackie waved the bread knife at me. I scurried backward off her weeds, until my feet hit blacktop. There was no way Jackie's bread knife was going to make contact with me, not in a million years. But it seemed possible she might accidentally fall and impale herself on it. I didn't want that appearing in my personnel file.

"I don't want you to be scared of me, Ms. Willis. But we've had some complaints."

"That don't matter, you still can't trespass! If you do, I can stab you! Like that fella over in Pensacola."

I sighed. I knew that story would rear its ugly head among the Gulf Breeze citizenry sooner or later. A couple months earlier, a Pensacola code enforcement officer responding to a complaint had been attacked by a citizen with a meat cleaver. Pensacola was directly north of Gulf Breeze, on the other side of the Pensacola Bay. I knew the officer, Jim Shafer, well enough to say hey to. He was an okay guy, not overly macho—though all of the Pensacola code enforcement guys were burlier, and more macho, than me.

Jim had been responding to a resident's complaint about a neighbor's yard, just as I was doing now. When he arrived he found a yard full of junk, mostly broken baby strollers and high chairs mixed with broken and empty booze bottles, and weeds over two feet high, a clear violation of Section 4.3.16 of Pensacola's Municipal Code. As he headed up the walkway to knock on the door, the homeowner burst out of the house and began swinging at him with the cleaver.

Jim sustained injuries to his face and arm but was expected to make a full recovery. Still, the incident was dramatic enough to throw the whole code enforcement community nationwide into an uproar. Some cities immediately enrolled their code enforcement staff in self-defense classes. In other areas, staff demanded the right to carry firearms.

Locally, public sentiment leaned in favor of the crazy citizen with the cleaver, at least if the comments on the *Pensacola News Journal* website were any indication. They were largely of a "damn trespasser got what he deserved" variety. Not surprising, given that this is the Florida Panhandle, where the norm is a strong distaste for authority (apparent even among the many residents who are retired military) combined with a respect for private property that borders on worship. No doubt this prevailing sentiment is where Ms. Willis got her notion that the cleaver guy had the law on his side. She'd skipped over the part where he'd been taken into custody and charged with several felonies.

My boss, Mike Jones, is a city slicker from Atlanta who doesn't share the Panhandle view of things. When news of the attack on Jim broke, Mike was so concerned he called me at home to ask if I wanted to start carrying a weapon on code enforcement calls. If so, he assured me, The Chief would expedite a concealed weapon permit. They weren't even going to wait for Council approval. All I had to do was say the word.

I'd laughed him off the phone. Now, though, looking at the business end of Jackie Willis's bread knife, I wondered if I'd been too hasty in dismissing the idea of a gun.

"Git, you!" Jackie said, waving the knife around again. "Shoo!"

I pictured myself hoisting out a Glock, taking a *Charlie's Angels* stance, and ordering Jackie to "Drop the bread knife!" The thought made me giggle.

Unfortunately, the sight of me giggling seemed to push Jackie over some kind of edge.

"Don't you laugh at me, Blondie!" she shrieked, and she actually took a step down off the porch. This was my signal to retreat. But I paused at the sight of Jackie swaying unsteadily on the top step. Self-impalement seemed imminent. She finally regained her balance, though she promptly endangered herself again by taking another step down, a move that was followed by more violent wobbling.

"I'll send you a letter!" I yelled, darting over to my city-issued F-150 and hopping up into the cab. I had time to snap a quick picture of the weedy yard before driving away. Just for good measure, I took one of Jackie and her bread knife, too. In case there was an impalement later, I'd have evidence that it was self-inflicted.

"That's right, Blondie! You'd better run!" I heard Jackie cry as I drove down Joachim Street.

I made a right onto Daniel Drive and a beeline for the Starbucks. It was a little early for a break. But I thought having a knife pulled on one—even if it was only a bread knife—warranted an early break.

"Hey, Gail," a tinny voice said as I pulled up to the squawk box. I recognized the voice of Jamie Bonner, my favorite barista. We'd graduated from Gulf Breeze High together six years ago. I'd once played Juror 7 to his Juror 8 in a production of *12 Angry Jurors*.

I waved at the security camera. "The usual?" Jamie asked.

"With a coffee cake."

I pulled up to the window. "Breakfast of Champions," Jamie said, handing me my cake and a napkin.

"A resident pulled a knife on me. I'm reevaluating some life decisions. I need extra carbs."

"There's always a place for you at Starbucks," Jamie said, handing me my latte.

I pulled the truck out of the drive-thru and into one of the parking spaces facing Highway 98, then cut the engine.

I stared moodily at the commuter traffic while I ate my coffee cake. It's not as though Junior City Planner for the City of Gulf Breeze, Florida, had been first choice for what I wanted to be when I grew up. First choice had been relief pitcher and team captain for the New York Yankees. But starting pitcher and team captain for the FSU Lady Seminoles softball team was as close as I'd come to that dream before the realities of anatomy set in. When I made starter during my freshman year, I told my teammates I was going to cut off my right breast, like an Amazon, so I could make it to the Majors. But by sophomore year I realized I liked The Girls too much to part with one.

When I saw that the NCAA Championships were as far as my athletic abilities would take me, I looked around for Plan B. I found it on the night a date dragged me to a guest lecture at the university by Elizabeth Plater-Zyberk, a Miami-based architect and pioneer of New Urbanism. To my surprise—not to mention my date's—I found myself interested in what she had to say. After that night I dumped the date but set my sights on an Urban Planning degree.

For the next two years, as I completed my classes, I imagined myself designing neighborhoods that were walkable and friendly, with parks and bike paths so appealing they would draw people out from behind their 6-foot privacy fences and back into the community again. Kids would get out of the house and play, instead of staring at a TV screen all day. It would be a revolution, though not one fought with shouting or picket signs or ugly words. Instead, my work would be so enticing the strip malls would simply disappear.

But now, instead of planning idyllic communities, I was getting cutlery waved at me by citizens who were too disorganized, or too crazy, to mow their own lawns.

Not that I blamed Jackie. She could barely take care of herself; taking care of her lawn was beyond her ability. But instead of helping her out, her neighbors in the big house next door called the city and filed a complaint about her.

I looked inside the little Starbucks bag, but there was nothing left. I'd finished my cake and I was still grumpy. This was bad.

I considered going back through the drive-thru and getting a donut. But all of a sudden I realized I was looking at a Gulf-BreezeSingles.com sign. It was planted in the grass of the Highway 98 median. I'd been looking at it the whole time, but I was so flustered by the Jackie Willis thing it had taken this long to register.

"Maggie freaking Gyllenhaal," I muttered, climbing out of my truck and stomping over to the curb. I snapped a picture of the sign with my phone, then waited for a break in traffic to dash out to the median, yank up the sign, and scurry back to the truck, where I tossed it into the bed. Then I got back in the cab and emailed the photo to my coworker, Emily Wright. Just for good measure, I included the picture of Jackie Willis with the knife, too.

A moment later the phone rang.

"Wtf, Mate?" Emily said when I answered.

"Ms. Willis is exercising the right to bear arms to protect her weedy yard."

"Spiffy. I see you found a GulfBreezeSingles sign, too."

"Yup. On 98, in front of the Starbucks."

"Starbucks, eh?"

"I had a knife pulled on me. I needed refreshment."

"Understandable. We just got a call that more signs were spotted out by the Seashore."

"Which side?"

"South side of 98, and also in the Visitors' Center parking lot."

"I'm on my way."

"Bring me a chai!"

I disconnected, drained the last of my latte, and put the truck in gear. The drive-thru line was now wrapped around the building, so I skipped Emily's chai and turned onto 98. She preferred her chai hot, and it would be cold by the time I got back to the office.

One of my code enforcement duties is upholding Gulf Breeze's sign ordinance. And Gulf Breeze takes its sign ordinance very seriously. At least, it does now. The city was incorporated in 1961 but didn't really form a strong opinion about signs until the late '80s. That's when our famous UFO sightings occurred. On November 17, 1987, the *Gulf Breeze Sentinel* published the account of Ed Walters, a local building contractor who said his front yard had been visited by a UFO and he had the pictures to prove it. The national UFO community quickly picked up the story, and within a few weeks Gulf Breeze was inundated with visitors hoping to catch a glimpse of the visitors.

Instantly a UFO cottage industry sprang up. Before long, Highway 98 had become one endless, homemade advertisement offering photos, tours, anecdotes, souvenirs and personal introductions to the aliens.

The Town Fathers were appalled. Their vision for Gulf Breeze, which had remained somewhat hazy for the better part of three decades, suddenly snapped into sharp focus. They wanted Gulf Breeze to be the shining gem of the Emerald Coast, as our stretch of the Gulf is called by marketers, though locals know it by its real name: the Redneck Riviera.

Well, so be it. Gulf Breeze might be located smack in the middle of the Redneck Riviera, but that didn't mean the Town Fathers were going to give in to handmade signs with crooked lettering inviting tourists to take home a sample of GENUINE MARTIAN SEAMEN.

They wanted something different. Something classy. Maybe even quaint. True, the past 25 years of development had allowed the 98 corridor to become a bit of an eyesore. But from now on, they were putting their feet down. Not to economic growth, but to poor taste. Gulf Breeze would be the Provincetown of the Redneck Riviera, or die trying.

City Council rewrote the commercial section of the development code. As soon as it was ratified, the Mayor went out to Highway 98 and personally removed the WELCOME E.T.! signs, bringing a photographer from the *News Journal* with him to document how serious Gulf Breeze was about classing the place up.

When Mike joined the city staff as Community Development Director a dozen years later, he went even further. Mike has a passion for Italianate architecture and a genius for writing

13

municipal ordinances. By the time he was through with it, Gulf Breeze had one of the tightest sign laws in the country.

What did this mean for me? Basically it meant I was the neighborhood killjoy. I'd drive around the city twice a week pulling up illegally placed yard sale and real estate signs. If the perpetrators called to find out where their signs had gone, I'd read the ordinance to them and explain how they could go about applying for a legal sign permit. It was usually too late for the yard sales, but sometimes the realtors would come in, cursing me under their breath as they filled out the paperwork and paid the fee.

And then, about a year ago, I was driving into work one morning when I saw it, planted by the curb in front of the Costmart parking lot. (Yes, we have a Costmart. But it's disguised behind such a mass of corbels, cornices, and cupolas, you'd hardly recognize it.)

Need a Date?
GulfBreezeSingles.COM

My first GulfBreezeSingles sign. It was an innocuous enough thing: plain white corkboard, 2 feet by 3 feet, with metal legs that could be driven into the dirt to stand up just about anywhere. The text was plain black lettering. Yet this simple sign—and the hundreds of others like it that followed over the next several months—had been enough to drive Mike nearly to drink. And Mike is normally a sober, sober man.

By the time I hauled that first GulfBreezeSingles sign into the office, residents had called to report five more of them, scattered around town. The next day, there were 10. And so it went, for several months. At the height of the madness, it seemed like every time I removed one of the signs, three others would sprout up in its place. And this is a city with less than five square miles of land area! The pile of signs next to the city's utility shed—

Mike had ordered me not to throw them away—grew as high as the shed itself.

As the weeks went by and the signs continued to proliferate, Mike became obsessed. He was Captain Ahab, and those signs were his Moby Dick. In my role as Starbuck, the voice of reason, I tried to persuade Mike to cool his jets a little. When it got to the point that chasing after the signs all day was putting me behind in my other work, I suggested maybe it wouldn't be the end of the world if some of the signs sat in place for a few days. I could go out a couple afternoons a week to catch up on sign removal. And eventually the company that was guilty of producing and placing the signs would be shut down, or they would simply give up on us. It was impossible to believe they were making any money on a dating site for Gulf Breeze residents. The median age in Gulf Breeze is around 150 years old. Jackie Willis is a hot dating prospect in Gulf Breeze. We would just ride it out until the perpetrators gave up.

Instead of listening to my wisdom, Captain Ahab hired himself a Flask—the toadying assistant who fuels his boss's obsession. Our Flask's name was Shawn O'Brien. I wasn't even sure how Mike got away with hiring him so quickly. Normally hiring someone at the city was sort of like enacting a Constitutional amendment. You had to put things in the paper and interview at least 37 people and give them tests and whatnot. But Mike must have evoked some obscure sign emergency clause in the municipal code, because I walked into the office one morning in the midst of the sign crisis and there was Shawn.

Mike promptly put me in charge of him. I didn't want to be in charge of him. He looked a little weaselly to me. But there was nothing to be done. I was now supervising my first employee.

Shawn was one of those short, stocky guys whose arms don't hang straight down at his sides. Well, that wasn't really his fault.

But he also had an enormous mustache, regarding which he had no one to blame but himself. Worst of all, he was fond of regaling everyone at the office with tales of his marital bliss.

Don't get me wrong, I don't begrudge anyone domestic happiness. In fact, I applaud it. My own married life is simple and happy. (More on this later.) But Shawn's method of proving that his home life was idyllic was to describe the long, steamy showers he and his wife took together. To me, this just seemed like an excuse to talk dirty at the office. Also, despite his constant allusions to the perfect sexual communion that was his marriage, Shawn had a tendency to stare hungrily at me whenever he came to the office to discuss "sign strategy," which he did much more often than the topic warranted.

Dude, you're the part-time sign guy. There is no sign strategy. Get out there, pull those suckers up, add them to the pile by the shed. That's your strategy.

I kept my opinion to myself, though, because I could see Shawn was all that was standing between Mike and a nervous breakdown. It was why Mike was willing to overlook the shower talk, which normally would have skeeved him out even more than it did me. But the weeks passed and the signs continued to proliferate. Mike became desperate. He got special permission from Patrick, our city manager, to purchase a couple of Nanny-cams, which he had Shawn install in high-traffic areas where signs had repeatedly shown up. After that, in addition to his sign-collecting duties, Shawn would go out and change the memory cards on the cameras twice a week. Each time he brought the memory cards back to the office, Mike was there to meet him. He'd snatch the cards and scurry back to his office, where he eagerly perused the images captured by the cameras, sure that this time he would have his man. But the cameras never captured anything except the Breezers, shopping and going about their business during the day, and raccoons at night.

When the cameras didn't pan out, Mike decided one of us needed to go on the GulfBreezeSingles site and create a dating profile. He thought we'd get more information about the company that way.

For some reason, I was nominated for this duty. Personally I thought Shawn should have been the one—was he the sign guy, or what?—but I didn't push the issue. Fortunately, my husband Chris has a good sense of humor. But even this sacrifice didn't amount to much. The only additional information we got out of my online profile was the name of the Internet Service Provider hosting the site. Once we had that, we were able to find a business address, of sorts—a P.O. Box in New Mexico. And once we had *that*, Mike fired off a scathing cease-and-desist letter threatening legal action.

After sending his letter, Mike relaxed visibly for the first time in months, confident the wheels of justice were in motion. I wasn't so sure. The web hosting company was clearly some sort of black-hat ISP. Its other clients were probably spammers and child pornographers. It seemed unlikely that a nastygram from some podunk town on the Florida Panhandle would even raise the pulse of the ISP's lawyers.

But shortly after that, the signs started to taper off. Mike was jubilant, believing his letter was the source of this victory. I thought my original theory, that there was no profit to be made from a dating website for Gulf Breeze, was more likely. Regardless of the cause, life started to return back to normal.

I even started thinking maybe I would finally be rid of Shawn. But I could kiss that dream goodbye now, if the signs were reappearing.

About a mile into the Seashore, just before the entrance to the Visitors' Center, I saw the first sign Emily had mentioned. I pulled over onto the shoulder of the road and hopped out to grab it, then started the truck again and pulled into the Visitors'

Center parking lot.

"The Seashore," as it's known to locals, is the Gulf Islands National Seashore, specifically the small portion of it that runs through Gulf Breeze. The Seashore is part of the national park system. Designated a protected landscape by the National Park Service in 1971, it runs in intermittent chunks along the coast of the Florida Panhandle, skips over Alabama, and then continues along the barrier islands of Mississippi.

The portion of the Seashore located in Gulf Breeze includes the Naval Live Oaks Reservation, a tract of land the U.S. government used before the Civil War "to experiment in growing live oaks from acorns." Or so says an information plaque at the Visitors' Center.

What else would they grow live oaks from? I wondered, each time I read the plaque. I'd been wondering for 20 years. To date no one had been able to supply an answer for me.

The Navy had cultivated the live oaks for shipbuilding. But iron had long ago replaced wood as the primary material in shipbuilding, in turn to be replaced by steel. The Live Oaks Visitors' Center was one of those places where you could learn about an obscure piece of Americana. You could read about the acorns, hoist a block of live oak wood to feel how much denser it was than other woods, and take an easygoing hike through the forest to the shore of the Santa Rosa Sound.

Looking across the parking lot I could see that Emily's intel was correct: there were a few more of the dating site signs sunk into the grass next to a walking path. Their placement here at the Visitors' Center was odd. If the dating site was paying some local schmuck to plant these signs around town, surely its intent was that the signs would be placed in high-traffic areas. As high traffic as anything ever got in sleepy little Gulf Breeze, anyway.

Up until now, the signs we found had more or less followed that line of reasoning. Most often they'd clustered in commercial areas—by the supermarkets, at the high school, in front of the churches. The one in front of Starbucks was typical.

I still couldn't believe the online dating service was making any money from the denizens of Gulf Breeze, but putting signs in the Live Oaks Visitors' Center parking lot represented a new low. There were never any visitors at the Visitors' Center. The parking lot was always empty, except for the trucks the Park Rangers drove and a few others belonging to local fishermen. And the fishermen weren't there for the acorn plaque or the live oaks. They were there for the free public access boat ramp. They never even set foot in the Visitors' Center.

I headed across the parking lot to the walking path, yanked the first sign out of the ground, tucked it under my arm, and continued over to the next one. I did the same with the second and was on my way to the final sign when something about the second one gave me pause. I untucked it and looked at it closely for the first time.

Mitagate?
PanhandleForChange.COM

This was new, and I was pretty sure it had nothing to do with online dating. I'd never heard of Panhandle for Change, but *Panhandlers* for Change was a local grassroots organization that had sprung up after the last election. Emily at the office belonged, which was the only reason I knew the group existed. (Whenever she was quizzed about the group's preposterous name, Em's mouth got very small, and she tersely declared that she had not been involved in name selection.) Could this sign have something to do with her group? If so, we were going to have words. Emily knew better than to mess with the sign ordinance. I approached the final sign with more interest.

Dawn Corrigan

Not too late?
WatershedBlog.COM

Very weird. Someone was riffing on the original GulfBreeze-Singles signs. Maybe this was some sort of advertising campaign cooked up by the Park Rangers? If so, I would have to put the signs back, as it wasn't a code violation for them to have the signs on park grounds. But if so, it was the lamest advertising campaign in history. Not to mention the most baffling. What exactly were they getting at?

I headed toward the Visitors' Center to have a word with the rangers when something made me stop in my tracks. It was a loggerhead turtle, lying in the grass directly to the right of the last sign. It was very unusual to see a loggerhead this far from the gulf beaches—they didn't get into the Sound too often. But the turtle clearly wasn't worried about being lost, I realized as I looked at it more closely. The turtle had bigger problems. The turtle was dead.

There was no way the park rangers had anything to do with this. Loggerheads are protected, and we Gulf Coast residents take our sea turtles very seriously.

I took out my cell phone and dialed Tad, aka "The Chief"—Gulf Breeze's Chief of Police. When I told him about the turtle he said he'd be right over. Then I called Emily. Em was one of our administrative assistants. Technically she didn't do fieldwork, but I wanted a little moral support. It was turning out to be a very strange morning. She said she'd be right over, too.

While I waited for them I crouched down to take a closer look at the loggerhead. It was an adolescent, with a carapace about a foot long. I'd seen baby loggerheads so small they could fit in the palm of my hand, and I'd seen adult mamas, three feet in length or more, coming ashore at night to lay their eggs. But normally one only ever saw sea turtles on land on those two oc-casions. All the time in between, which the loggerheads spend out at sea conducting their mysterious turtle business, is known as "the lost years." People on land weren't supposed to see foot-long loggerheads.

Especially not dead ones. Every summer of my childhood, my father and I had walked the beaches before dawn, looking for new sea turtle nests. When we found one, we would erect a temporary fence made from old bed sheets wrapped around stakes, which Keith kept in his truck bed just for this purpose. Then he would call the Park Service and report the nest location, so they could come out the next day to do a census of the nest and place an officially sanctioned Park Ranger fence around it.

The rangers knew my dad and would save his bed sheets for him so he could reuse the same ones. Which he did, summer after summer, until they disintegrated and had to be replaced.

The poor dead turtle looked like a sad little puppy, with its legs splayed out to the sides and its chin resting against the grass. It had the characteristic cocoa-colored spots on its head, legs, and shell, as well as the large head that gives the species its name. I reached out and rubbed the shell.

But when I felt myself starting to tear up, I stood back up. "Get a grip," I muttered.

"Boo!" a voice said near my ear. "Or should I say, 'Boo *hoo*'?" It was Emily, who'd arrived ahead of The Chief. I looked back toward the parking lot and saw her vintage yellow VW bug parked next to my truck. I'd been so absorbed in the turtle I hadn't even heard her pull up.

"Very funny. Anyway, I'm not crying. I got something in my . . . eyes."

"Oh sure," Emily said. "That happens." Emily is a tiny, myopic brunette. I tower over her. She squinted up at me as she removed her prescription sunglasses and rubbed them with a cleaning cloth. "Was the sight of yet another GulfBreezeSingles sign more than you could bear?"

"Yes. It offended my delicate planner's sensibility. But also, there was the turtle." I pointed at the ground next to the sign.

"Aww!" Emily squealed, squatting down next to the turtle. "Hey," she added almost immediately. "This turtle is dead! You didn't tell me it was dead!" She stood back up, shaking her head. Then her eyes fell on the Not too late? sign. "That's not a GulfBreezeSingles sign."

"Nope. This time we got two new messages."

"Let me see the other one."

I showed her the Mitagate? sign. "Someone from your group, maybe?"

"No way," Emily said, looking disturbed. "We're Panhand*lers* for Change. Plus, the perpetrator can't spell," she added, pointing at the word *Mitagate*. "PFC is comprised entirely of former spelling bee champs."

"I thought it looked funny." I hadn't really been sure, but I wasn't going to admit that now.

"Yeah. That 'a' should be an 'i.' Somebody's taking the name of my grassroots group in vain. There was one of the usual suspects here, too?"

"Yup." I showed her the Need a date? sign.

Emily studied the signs for a moment. "That one is the same as the 3,000 others we've already found," she said, pointing to the GulfBreezeSingles sign. "But these others are different. They're made from thinner material—a couple sheets of posterboard stuck together, it looks like. The writing is different, too. The Dating signs seem to be machine printed. These others were done by hand."

"Seriously?" They'd all looked the same to me.

"Yeah. Someone did a meticulous job of it, though—they really tried hard to match the font on the Dating signs. But you can see a few places where they squiggled a bit." Emily pointed to the first 'a' on the Mitagate sign.

She was right; there was a tiny shake on the bottom curve of the a. "I could have stared at this sign for a year and I wouldn't have noticed that," I said admiringly.

"It's nice to know my OCD is good for something."

The sound of Chief Tobin's car entering the parking lot caused us both to look up. As he drew closer, he flashed lights and siren for a moment, then the windows slid down. I saw David King, the city engineer, sitting beside The Chief up front.

"Mornin', ladies." Tad and David grinned up at us.

The Chief is Gulf Breeze's own Boss Hogg, though he's a Boss with a heart of gold. He has a big beer belly and a drawl and in all physical respects is the stereotype of the good old boy small-town sheriff. His behavior doesn't fit the stereotype, though. He's always giggling about something with David or with Patrick, the city manager. Usually it's something like the new AC/DC ringtone one of them has finally figured out how to download to his cell phone. They're like mischievous 12-year-old boys.

David, on the other hand, is a stereotypical engineer, meaning he wants to pave over everything that's green and messy in the world. Or so he likes to joke, mainly to get under the skins of Emily and Mike, our resident treehuggers on the city staff. Shortly after Emily started working with us, David printed out "The Pavers' Creed" from the Interwebs and hung it on the wall of his office, just to rile her up.

Now he leaned out the window to address his nemesis. "Should've known you'd be here, as soon as word got out there was a dead turtle on the scene."

"As government employees we should all be concerned about a loggerhead dying under mysterious circumstances," Emily responded primly. "It's a protected species."

"So you think the turtle was murdered?" David asked. "Is

this a hate crime?"

"Why don't you gentlemen get out of that air conditioning and come see for yourselves?"

The Chief stopped the engine and the men climbed out of the car. I showed them the signs and indicated where the first two had been positioned. I was sorry now that I'd pulled them up.

"These other two were constructed differently," The Chief observed.

"That's what Emily said."

The men bent down to examine the loggerhead.

"Poor little fella," David said.

"Probably a female, actually. They're the only ones that come back to shore after they're hatched."

"This one's too young to be laying eggs, though."

"So what's this guy up to?" David said. "Panhandle for Change," he added, examining the second sign. "Isn't that your group, Emily?"

She shrugged, looking troubled. "It's not our sign, and the name's not quite right, but it probably does refer to us. I think 'mitagate' must refer to mitigation banks. Our group has been researching them."

"Aha, so you're responsible for the poor turtle's death!"

"I'm not sure this was actually turtle murder," The Chief interjected. "The park rangers got a few calls yesterday about a dead loggerhead floating in the gulf waters out around Villa Sabine." Villa Sabine was a condo complex in West Pensacola Beach. "Mothers were calling in saying their kids were upset about it, that kind of thing. The callers all said it was about a foot long, like this one. But when the rangers went to pick it up, they couldn't find it."

"So someone snatched an already dead turtle out of the Gulf to use in conjunction with their incomprehensible and misspelled sign campaign?" Emily asked incredulously.

"Yeah," David chimed in. "And you'd think if they were going to go to all this trouble, they'd make the message a little clearer. I mean, what *is* the message here? Does anyone else get it? Am I the only thick one?"

We all looked around at each other. The Chief shrugged, and Emily and I shook our heads.

"Maybe the websites will give us a clue," I suggested.

"And I'll ask Karen Baretta," said Emily. "She's the one in Panhandlers for Change who knows the most about mitigation banks."

CHAPTER TWO

Karen and Joe were surprised to see that the eggs had hatched at nest number 47 when they arrived just before dawn that morning. They thought it was at least another week out. Even worse, the boil had already occurred. Unfortunately, the nest was so close to the Portofino Condominiums that half the hatchlings had headed up toward the beckoning lights of the condos, rather than toward the water.

Karen silently cursed herself, looking down at the homemade disorientation screen in her hand. It consisted of several car window shades she and Joe had duct taped together and affixed to wire posts. They had planned to place it around the nest that morning, to block the light from the condos so the baby turtles could get a bead on where the water was after hatching. They were obviously too late. To make matters worse, it was a new moon, so there was no moonlight reflecting off the water to guide the babies. As a result they were scattered everywhere.

Twenty years or more after hatching, female loggerheads return to land, often to the beach where they were born. Arriving at night, they drag their 300-pound selves up the beach into the dunes, dig a hole, and lay 100 or more eggs in it, then cover the hole with sand and return to the water. They'll stay in coastal waters during nesting season and may return to land once or twice more to nest again, but they never return to a nest once the eggs are laid.

Left to their own devices, the eggs incubate for anywhere

26

from 50 to 70 days. When they start hatching, the nest caves in—this is how observers can tell the action is starting. Because it's turtles we're talking about, the action takes awhile to heat up. After the cave-in not much happens at first. Then, anywhere from 8 to 36 hours later, the babies come pouring out of the sand all at once and make a mad dash for the water. They look like lava boiling out of a volcano. Hence the nickname for this moment, the "boil."

Karen and Joe had checked this nest the previous morning and it had still been intact. That meant both the cave-in and the boil had occurred sometime within the past 20 hours.

Judging from the evidence, it had been very recent. Joe had already located some babies not too far from the nest and was tracking their progress. The group he'd found had managed to point themselves toward the water. He didn't interrupt them in their scramble toward the shore, but he did stand guard, ready to stave off any gulls or crabs that might consider making one of the hatchlings breakfast. He walked with funny mincing steps, not wanting to squish one of his charges. He couldn't use a flashlight, as that would further exacerbate the already fubar situation regarding the light.

Loggerhead babies hatch and emerge from their nests at night, prompted by the sand's cooler temperatures. Ideally, they head straight toward the ocean (or gulf—the nearest big body of salt water, anyway). Moonlight and starlight reflected off the water clue them in as to which way they're supposed to go. The problem is, they're hard wired to head for the brightest light. If a condo complex is competing with starlight, the condo often wins, and the turtle babies will go scrambling in exactly the wrong direction, until they're eaten, or run over, or the sun comes up and they simply give in to heat and exhaustion.

Karen went after the poor little buggers that had headed toward the false dawn of the condos. When she'd collected five of them she turned and started for the water, passing Joe and his herding efforts as she went.

"Are you going to carry them all the way down?" There was a note of disapproval in Joe's voice. "The walk **actually** strengthens them for swimming later, you know."

"Oh, cram it," his wife said affably, wading into the Gulf. "They'll face plenty of other tests of their mettle soon enough." When the water was up to her thighs she **bent** and set the turtles gently on its surface. They immediately **began** paddling like mad. She watched as they swam off. Only one in a thousand would make it to adulthood.

When she turned back to search for more stragglers, Joe was kicking sand at a ghost crab that was eyeballing his charges. "Git," he said. The crab scuttled into one of its holes, but almost immediately scuttled back out.

"That crab wants turtle meat for breakfast, no doubt about it," Karen said, heading back up the beach. She quickly found five more babies and carried their wiggling selves down to the water. Joe *tsk-tsk*ed at her as she passed. "It's crawling across the sand that teaches them about the earth's magnetic fields," he said. "Your turtles won't have any sense of direction."

"They'll manage," Karen said. "After all, you do fine without one."

By this point most of Joe's group had reached the water. "I hope that ghost crab doesn't just follow them in," he said, watching the crawlers as they launched themselves into the sea.

"There's more where he came from," Karen said. "Will your scruples allow you to help me look for more Wrong Ways now? And how many did you have?"

"Seventeen."

"That's it? C'mon, let's go look for more." Karen hurried back up the beach, Joe trailing behind her. Twenty-seven hatchlings would be a disappointing total from a nest that might hold as many as 125 eggs. After the boil she and Joe were supposed to dig up the nest and count the total number of eggs, the unhatched eggs, and the number of hatchlings that had died before making it to the surface and report their findings to Florida Fish and Wildlife. Sometimes the total number of eggs was known in advance because sometimes the nests were moved. If the female turtle dug her nest too close to the waterline, volunteers would dig a replica nest farther up the beach, then painstakingly move the eggs to the new location. But this mama had done a good job with nest placement, so she and Joe hadn't needed to do anything besides marking the location and keeping watch for the past two months.

When a nest was inventoried after a boil, there were always a few dead hatchlings. They always broke Karen's heart. After she and Joe did another sweep for any misdirected stragglers, maybe she would dig up the nest and see if there were any hatchlings buried alive under the sand, then sneak them down to the water.

Joe would say that was the wrong thing to do. He would argue that any hatchlings not strong enough to make it to the surface weren't supposed to live, and that she wasn't doing the *Caretta caretta* gene pool any favors by saving them. But she didn't care. The turtles experienced enough hardship, much of it a result of human interference. Even for those who managed to escape the condo lights there was the risk of swallowing a plastic bag, which many sea turtles and other marine creatures did, mistaking them for jellyfish. And don't even get her started on the shrimp nets.

But humans weren't the only creatures that made life a constant struggle for the sea turtles. There were also the ghost crabs and the sea gulls and the sharks. Karen saw nothing wrong with giving the turtles a leg up.

Though she and Joe searched extensively, they were only able to find three more hatchlings crawling among the dunes. One of them had gotten dangerously close to the road when Joe found it. This caused Karen to go right out into the road and look around, in case any babies had made it all the way to the blacktop.

Karen handed Joe her turtles. Suppressing his scruples, he carried them down to the water to please his wife while she returned to the nest to start digging for buried hatchlings.

"Karen, what are you doing over there? I have a bad feeling about this," he said as he walked back toward the shore.

"Never you mind," she said. Shaking his head ruefully at his tenderhearted wife, Joe waded into the water and released the three tiny turtles.

When he got back to the nest, Karen was gone.

CHAPTER THREE

Rosario started waving message slips in the air the moment we walked in the office. "For you," she said to Emily, handing her five slips, "and for you," handing me two. I sensed a note of disapproval in her voice. Rosario was the other administrative assistant in our department, in addition to Emily. She didn't like it when I lured Emily out of the office. In Rosario's philosophy, admins were supposed to stay chained to their desks.

Rosario Gardner covered Building and Public Works. She was in her mid-50s, tall and slender, with extremely upright posture and short, frosted hair. She spoke with a thick Southern purr that masked an iron core, her true disposition.

"What does this mean—'Resident wants to complain about golfers golfing at golf course?' " Emily asked, reading her first slip.

"Ooh, that one's a doozy."

"But what does he want?"

Rosario smiled wickedly. "He wants you to make them stop golfing."

Emily sighed as she slipped into her chair and picked up the phone. As I headed back to my office, I heard her say, "May I speak with Mr. Dalton, please?" in her most patient voice.

The city offices were split across two buildings. The main building housed the office of Patrick Gribble, the City Manager, and his admin Stacy Holmes, as well as the Controller, the Recorder, Parks & Recreation, and Krista Black, who handled

Traffic Court Administration. Though the Mayor's position was only part time, he had a desk there as well.

My department, Community Development, was located in an annex to the east. The annex was a 1970s split-level. On the upper level was the conference room where City Council and Planning Commission meetings were held, as well as the weekly Traffic Court sessions. The lower floor opened into a reception area that had a long counter where staff could unroll building plans or development plats for review, as well as a couple of round tables where visitors could sit to fill out our many application forms. Emily and Rosario had workstations directly behind the long counter.

On the north side of Emily's desk there was a hallway that led back to the kitchen, the supply room, and the offices of David, Mike and me. This arrangement gave us the option to stay hidden from the public until summoned by Emily or Rosario.

It also gave me the chance to duck out of sight when Rosario was on a tear. You didn't want to cross Rosario. She was older than most of the city staff, except for Patrick and the Mayor, and had worked for the city longer than any of us. She was also a lifelong resident of Gulf Breeze who knew virtually every resident by name, as well as the complicated webs of gossip and intrigue that wove them all together. For all these reasons, she was a little intimidating.

Though I felt a pang of sympathy for Emily, I was glad for the chance to hide in my own office during moments like these, when Rosario let her displeasure with us be known.

But once I reached my office, I found my situation wasn't much improved. My notes from Rosario were both messages from residents of the Yellow Tree subdivision. The second one was marked URGENT.

I didn't need to ask what they were calling about. It was yet another violation of the weed ordinance. But the circumstances were different in Yellow Tree than in Jackie Willis's yard.

The saga of the Yellow Tree development began before I came to work for the city. The subdivision was approved by Gulf Breeze's City Council in early 2006, when the local housing bubble was still intact. The boom had risen to even more frenzied heights here on the panhandle than in many comparable areas of the country because of the back-to-back hits of Hurricanes Ivan and Dennis in September 2004 and July 2005. The two storms took out so much housing stock in our area that everything left standing was quickly snatched up by buyers with insurance money in their pockets. Ivan alone destroyed more than 7,000 homes. The occupancy rate for units still standing quickly reached 100 percent. Then the developers swooped in with a flurry of new projects hastily cobbled together.

Yellow Tree was one of these. It was an open space development calling for 55 homes to be built in several phases. Phase I was begun immediately after City Council granted final approval, and the first 22 houses were erected quickly. A dozen families moved into the new neighborhood in 2007.

Then the bottom fell out. By the time the city hired me in August 2007, the stream of requests for building permits had slowed to a trickle—not just for the Yellow Tree subdivision, but for every neighborhood in the city. Once the hurricane dust settled, it became clear that in Gulf Breeze, as in the rest of the country, there wasn't enough capital left to build an outhouse, let alone the 33 remaining houses of an unfinished subdivision.

By 2008, when the insurance money was spent and the national economy was crashing, there were dozens of new houses and condos in Pensacola Beach and Gulf Breeze and no one who could afford to buy or even rent them. Residents no longer materialized at our office with bundles of rolled-up architectural drawings tucked under their arms, eager to have their plans approved. Rosario's phone stopped ringing. She caught up on three years' worth of filing, having nothing else to do.

With two plats of Yellow Tree still left unbuilt, Dan Bradford, the developer, stopped coming by the city offices. Then Rosario reported a rumor that he'd skipped town altogether, leaving behind millions in debt.

Alongside the dozen occupied homes of Yellow Tree, Phase I, were 10 other houses that had been constructed but never sold. Those lots hadn't been landscaped, so they were surrounded by dirt. As summer wore on, the vacant houses with their dirt lots looked more and more forlorn, especially when compared to the flourishing yards of the occupied homes. Trash and debris blew into the unlandscaped lots and collected there. Pools of standing water formed, bringing mosquitoes. Then weeds began to take root. And with no one to control them, they quickly spread from the vacant lots to the yards of the occupied houses.

Now it was war. Everyone knows you don't mess with a subdivision dweller and his lawn. The residents of Yellow Tree were incensed. Banding together, they formed a committee, the Yellow Tree Committee to Uphold Covenants and Restrictions. Their elected chair and vice chair contacted the city to demand a meeting. In my capacity as Code Enforcement Officer, I was instructed by Mike to meet with them.

On the appointed day, they arrived 20 minutes early. Emily scurried into my office, announcing their presence with a hiss and asking if I wanted her to wait until the top of the hour to bring them in. I told her to show them back immediately. When she did they turned out to be a Mr. Crable and a Ms. Thompson, chair and vice chair, respectively. Mr. Crable was in his mid-50s, a retired military man who still kept the crewcut and the muscles. Ms. Thompson was about 10 years younger, the married, harried mother of two teenage daughters.

They were about ready to burst, they were so eager to tell me their story. I already knew the story, of course, and I knew they weren't going to like my response. I let the meeting play itself out, though. I let them talk. That was the mistake Mike and some of the other city staffers tended to make when they interacted with the public. They thought the object was to drive the conversation toward its conclusion as soon as possible. The real object, of course, is to let people talk themselves out.

Crable and Thompson talked for more than half an hour, interrupting each other at various intervals. Mr. Crable in particular had a genius for detail. He gave the Latin genus and species names, as well as the common names, for some of the weeds that were growing in the vacant Yellow Tree lots. He'd noted exact dates for the formation of a certain stagnant puddle, the appearance of a floating plastic bag.

After half an hour they started to wind down. By then they'd talked for so long they didn't know how to stop. They repeated what they felt were their most salient points several times. They were waiting for me to interrupt them, but I wasn't going to join the conversation unless invited. Finally Crable stopped repeating himself and made it a dialogue by asking a question. "What is the city going to do about the situation?"

I launched into one of my patented Urban Planning 101 speeches, explaining that when a subdivision was being constructed, the developer remained responsible for maintaining the property up to code until the lots were sold. Often, however, developers sold unbuilt lots to one or more builders after final approval was received and improvements were completed. In such cases, the builders were responsible for maintaining the lots.

In the case of Yellow Tree, the developer and the builder were one and the same: Dan Bradford. I would head up to Yellow Tree to take some pictures that very afternoon, I assured them. Then I would write to Mr. Bradford, informing him that his lots were in violation of city ordinance.

And what then? They wanted to know.

Mr. Bradford would have 10 days to bring the lots into compliance.

And if he didn't?

I would issue him a citation, with fines.

And then?

The city would work to enforce the citation.

I could feel their growing disgust. I think they were hoping the city would send a couple of public works guys right on over to weed the empty lots for them. Instead, they were getting a civics lesson from Blondie about the reality of upholding local ordinances, which requires the participation of citizens if it's going to work.

I was sorry to disappoint them, but that's how it goes. Besides, if I were going to send out a city employee to maintain privately owned lots, the Yellow Tree people could get in line. The Jackie Willises of the world needed help much more than these people. They were able-bodied; with all the time they'd put into their YRC meetings, they could have all the vacant lots in Yellow Tree weeded and seeded by now.

But I kept these thoughts to myself as I delivered my speech.

When I was finished Crable asked me, "Would it be all right for us to contact the developer directly?"

I allowed my face to brighten with approval. "I think that would be an excellent idea," I enthused. "The city will do what it can, but it's possible Mr. Bradford will be more responsive to you. After all, you were his clients."

They both stared at me blankly. They'd worked directly with Bradford when designing and building their homes, but they hadn't yet seemed to put it together that we were now talking about the same guy. They couldn't reconcile the man who'd spun fairy-tale visions of their dream homes with the person who was now responsible for their neighborhood deteriorating into a suburban blight area.

Even before Yellow Tree, Bradford had been known around the Community Development office for his upselling, as well as his tendency to use the cheapest materials possible. But he worked fast, and everything he built looked flashy on the surface, so clients loved him. Then, later, when the houses settled and their foundations cracked, or the plywood underpinning all the cabinets warped, those clients would call our office, full of ire.

"You'll need to contact the builder," Rosario would explain.

"But your inspector signed off on it!"

"The city's inspection is designed to ensure that the house was built to code, and that it's safe for occupancy. It's not a guarantee of the quality of workmanship. If you feel the house doesn't match what was covered by your contract with the builder, that might be a discussion to have with your attorney."

Indignant sputtering would ensue. For some reason, most residents preferred to focus their wrath on the city, rather than directing their anger back to the guy who'd understood their desires so perfectly, who'd known just how to bring their fantasy to life—the guy who'd actually built their shabby house.

The Yellow Tree residents fell into this group. They simply couldn't believe Bradford had abandoned them to their fate. If I was impatient with them, it was probably because I was predisposed against Yellow Tree in the first place. It represented everything I disliked in urban design: oversize houses built out to every square inch of the setbacks, constructed from inferior materials, and surrounded by hulking privacy fences. But, different strokes for different folks. The bottom line was, they just wanted to live someplace nice and were sad their neighborhood was falling into disrepair so quickly.

We were lucky there weren't more Yellow Trees in the city.

Elsewhere in the country thousands of subdivisions were in this condition. South Florida had been hit especially hard.

After our initial meeting, I provided Crable and Thompson with regular updates on their case. As I expected, Bradford ignored my original cease-and-desist letter, as well as the citation. We'd already marked up the fine once. What difference did it make? The guy was in the wind. You could make the fine $100 billion, he still wasn't going to show his face or turn up to weed those lots. If things didn't get resolved soon, it would be up to the HOA to increase its dues so it could pay for maintenance of the unoccupied units. I wasn't looking forward to introducing that notion to the Yellow Tree folks.

That left composing a letter to Jackie Willis. Out of the frying pan, into the fire.

I took out my cell phone and forwarded the two pictures of Jackie to my work email address. I only needed the one of her weedy yard for work purposes—I would print a copy and send it to her along with my cease-and-desist letter. The other picture, of Jackie waving the bread knife around, was strictly for my pleasure.

I pulled up my "Weed Notice" letter template and quickly added Jackie's name and address, the date of the neighbor's complaint, and the date of my onsite visit. When I was finished I skimmed it to make sure the template didn't say anything inappropriate to the situation. "It's come to our attention," "you may not be aware," "the relevant section of the Gulf Breeze development code," "if there are any mitigating circumstances the city should know about," yadda yadda yadda. Everything was in order. I printed the letter and the photograph, sealed them in an envelope, and addressed it to Jackie.

That was about all the desk work I could stand for the moment. I picked up the phone and dialed Emily's extension.

"Ms. Wright, may I see you in my office?"

Emily came in a moment later, shutting the door behind her. She had a notepad and pen clutched in her hand.

"What's up?" she asked, looking at me anxiously.

I had to laugh. Emily and I had become friends during the past year, but she would never stop treating me like the boss.

"Nothing. Don't get your panties in a bunch. I just want to check out those websites from the Visitor Center signs."

"Oh, okay," Emily said, looking relieved.

"What was up with that call about golfing that Rosario was going on about?"

"Edna St. Vincent Millay!" Emily exclaimed.

I should probably explain. Emily was originally from New Jersey, and when she first started working with us, she tended to pepper her speech with a lot of "Jesus, Mary and Josephs!" and "Oh my Gods!" She didn't mean any disrespect. It was just the way her people talked. It didn't bother me at all—in fact, I rather liked it. But then again, I hadn't exactly received the upbringing of a proper Southern belle. For a lot of southerners, that kind of language was just plain offensive.

At the end of Emily's first week on the job, Mike had called her into his office. He explained that such language didn't sit well with the good denizens of Gulf Breeze, where it was still considered taking the Lord's name in vain. If she was going to work for the city, she would have to find another way to talk.

She came to my office directly after leaving Mike's. Blinking away tears, she said she didn't think she could give up interjections altogether—having grown up in an Italian family in New Jersey, they were too ingrained in her speech. She was horrified at the thought that she might have offended the Breezers—or Mike, or me, or any other coworker. She supposed she would have to start looking for another job. She hoped Mike would let her stay on until she found something else.

Handing her a tissue, I assured her she certainly hadn't offended me, and I doubted she'd offended Mike, either. I said we could already tell she was going to be the best admin the department had ever seen, and Mike had no intention of firing her. (I had a pretty good idea who *was* offended—or at least, who had pretended to be offended, in order to stir the pot. It was the person who was now relegated to being the *second* best admin our department had ever seen, I was sure. But I kept that theory to myself.) Mike was just trying to look out for her best interests, since obviously she was still getting used to our Southern ways.

I asked Em if she couldn't learn to mince her swear words a little.

She wiped her eyes, then blew her nose into the tissue. "You mean like . . . Jesus, Mary and Glavin?"

I laughed. "That's no good. You left Jesus in. Could you say, maybe, 'Jiminy Cricket'?"

Emily smiled wanly. "I don't think so."

"Well then how about 'crikey'?" I persisted.

She started to giggle. "Gadzooks!" she cried.

"Zounds!"

We both cracked up just as Mike stuck his head in the door. He looked at the two of us, shook his head, and disappeared again.

The next day, Emily started using the names of famous writers to punctuate her speech. At least, she claimed they were famous. I didn't recognize most of them, though I could usually pick out the old-timey poets. ("John Greenleaf Whittier!" was a particular favorite.) Regardless, they made excellent expletives.

"I mean, David Foster Wallace!—was that guy nuts."

"David Foster Wallace?"

"No, the golf guy. Come to think of it, though, Wallace was a few peas short of a pod, too. He killed himself last year."

"Terrible."

"It was. But, the golf guy. A few months ago he bought one of those houses along the West 9 at Tiger Point. And now he's calling to complain that golfers are hitting golf balls too close to his house. He wants us to put a stop to it."

"He wants us to stop golfers from golfing on the golf course?"

"Yeah. He was about a million years old. Said a stray ball could hit him or his wife or his grandkids, who come to visit all the time."

"They always mention the safety of the children when they're asking for something completely unreasonable."

"Amen, Sista. I was so confused! For a while I thought maybe he meant certain golfers were aiming for his house *deliberately.* So I asked if that's what he meant. But that only seemed to make him madder."

"So, just to recap," I said, "of all the houses in Gulf Breeze, he chose to buy one right along the golf course. And now he wants us to make people stop golfing there."

"Your understanding of the situation is commendable," Emily said. "It's almost as though you've worked with the citizens of Gulf Breeze before. Boy, was he mad when I told him we couldn't make them stop golfing. He threatened to contact the media."

"Jennifer Love Hewitt!" I'd started responding to Emily's literary interjections by taking the names of B-list starlets in vain. "What did you say?"

"I told him that was a great idea."

"I can't wait to see him on the news tonight."

Emily sighed. "I'm sure he'll tell them all about how the City of Gulf Breeze, embodied in the form of one Emily Wright, was indifferent to his plight."

I laughed. "You are one cold-hearted admin. It's almost like you don't care about the safety of the children at all." I spun around toward my computer monitor. "Anyway, let's check out those websites. I assume you already know what the Panhandlers for Change site looks like. Just in case, I tried Panhandle forChange.com as well, but there's no such website, so I think the sign maker must have meant y'all. I also went back to Gulf BreezeSingles.com, but nothing's changed since I created my profile. So I figure we should start with the watershed blog."

I typed in the URL address while Emily came around and leaned on the desk behind me. A web page came up.

Thank you for visiting the Watershed Blog. There are over 2,000 watersheds in the contiguous United States of America, with 52 major ones in Florida alone. Wetlands are an integral part of watershed health. The loss of wetlands in our state has led to more coastal watershed flooding, resulting in millions of dollars in damage, not to mention lost lives.

Though wetlands are supposed to be protected by the Clean Water Act, we continue to lose thousands of acres of wetlands every year because of a travesty known as the MITAGATION BANK.

Many Florida Politicians, Planners, and Business Men are involved. Democrats and Republicans—both parties are guilty! Not to mention the EPA, Florida DOT, and even the U.S. Army Corps of Engineers!

Please ENTER the site to learn more about Watersheds, Wetlands, and Mitagation Banks.

There was a row of links along the top of the page: Watersheds, Wetlands, Mitagation Banks, Australia, Links, Contact Us. I clicked on Watersheds, but got a "Page Under Construction" message. The same was true for all the other links as well.

"Not much content on that site," Emily observed. "And someone needs to learn how to use spell check."

"He sounds like a real nut job." Then I quickly added, "No offense," thinking Emily probably agreed with the nut job.

But Em didn't argue. "Definitely. He starts out fairly rational, but quickly descends into conspiracy theorist territory. And can you say 'One of these links is not like the other'?"

I looked at the row of links again. "You mean Australia?"

"Yeah. What's up with that?"

I shrugged. "No idea. And since there's no content, we can't find out. Did your Panhandlers for Change group ever talk about Australia at all?"

"No." She stared at the screen for a moment, tugging on her lower lip. "I have an idea. Can I drive for a minute?"

"Sure." Emily leaned over and quickly typed something. A new browser window opened. She entered a URL, then typed something else and pressed Enter when the new page came up.

"Aha," she said after a moment.

"What?"

Em pointed at the screen. "This is a site that lets you find out what company hosts any website or blog."

"Oh. Cool." I wasn't sure why it was cool, but Em seemed pleased and I wanted to be supportive. I looked at the screen again. Evidently the watershed blog was hosted by a company named WebX3. "And this matters because . . . ?"

"The site is hosted by the same company that hosts the Gulf-BreezeSingles site."

"Huh. That's a weird coincidence—right?"

Emily smiled down at me. "Think about what a hard time we had finding the GulfBreezeSingles people. Whoever created this site wanted to make sure it was untraceable."

★ ★ ★ ★ ★

After Emily left I looked at my phone messages once more, then flopped my head down onto my desk. I still couldn't bring myself to pick up the phone and return the Yellow Tree calls.

I wondered if I needed to tell Mike I was getting a little burnt out on the code violation stuff.

I wondered if I could persuade Emily to return my calls for me.

I figured I probably could, even without inviting her to lunch. But I would invite her to lunch anyway because I wanted to get out of the office and talk more about the watershed blog. Plus, my taking Emily to lunch would piss off Rosario, and I was grumpy enough that pissing off Rosario seemed like a good idea.

I grabbed my message slips and headed out to the reception area.

Emily and Rosario both spun around in their chairs as I emerged. I casually leaned against the counter. I'd been planning on issuing my lunch invitation in a direct and firm manner, but now, meeting Rosario's eyes, I balked.

My mental scrambling for a Plan B was interrupted by a man staggering into the office. Small and slim, he looked to be in his late 60s. He was neatly dressed in belted khaki shorts, a collared shirt, and Tevas, but he looked drunk. He wheeled around, waving his arms in front of him in an effort to keep his balance. His white hair stuck out in tufts.

Then I noticed the gash in the back of his head, and the blood caked on his neck. Rosario gasped and Emily leapt to her feet and ran around to him. "Joe!" she exclaimed. "What happened?"

"It's Karen," he said. "She's been kidnapped. You've got to help," and he collapsed onto the office floor.

"Call 911," I said to Rosario. As soon as she picked up her

phone and started dialing, I took out my cell and called The Chief directly. After confirming that we'd already called the dispatcher, he said he'd be right over.

I hung up and went around the counter. Emily was crouching next to the man, who appeared to be unconscious. She had rolled him into the recovery position and had a hand on his wrist.

I kneeled beside her. "You know him?" I asked quietly.

Emily nodded. She looked very upset. "He and his wife Karen belong to PFC. Karen is the one I told you about earlier— our expert on mitigation banks." Our eyes met.

"And he said Karen had been kidnapped?" I asked incredulously. She nodded again. "Is there someone you can call?"

"I've been thinking about that. I suppose I could try calling Karen's number."

"Let's wait until The Chief gets here."

Fortunately we didn't have to wait long. About 30 seconds later he walked in.

"Ladies," he said quietly. We scurried out of the way as he lowered himself beside us. "Do we know his name?" he asked as his hands felt for a pulse.

"Joe Baretta."

"Mr. Baretta, can you hear me?"

The man opened his eyes. He winced, then stared ahead for a moment, then looked up at us. "Karen! Someone took Karen." He looked straight at The Chief. "Please do something!"

"We're going to find Karen, Mr. Baretta, I assure you of that. But first we need to get you some medical attention because it looks like someone banged you up pretty good. The paramedics should be here any moment now. I think they'd tell me I should just have you lie here quietly, but I'm going to let you tell me a little about what happened as long as you stay calm."

Joe never took his eyes off The Chief. "We were on turtle

patrol," he said. "One of the nests over by Portofino had boiled. Some of them went the wrong way. Karen was looking for strays. I carried some down to the water. When I got back to the nest I couldn't find her. Then someone must have hit me. When I woke up, she was gone."

"And how did you get here?"

"Drove." Em and I exchanged startled looks. We were a long way from the Portofino beaches. What had made him drive all the way here? Why hadn't he called someone as soon as he realized Karen was missing?

Joe must have sensed our confusion.

"I just kept thinking I had to get to the Gulf Breeze police station," he said. "But then I was afraid I was going to pass out, so I stopped here." The police station was about a mile farther up the road from the city office complex where we were located.

Just then the paramedics arrived. The Chief, Emily, and I stood up and got out of their way. I saw that Mike had come out of his office and was standing behind Rosario.

It didn't take the paramedics long to get Joe stabilized. As soon as they wheeled him out, The Chief got on his phone. From his side of the conversation I could tell he was talking to a sheriff out in Pensacola Beach. The beach was covered by the Escambia County sheriff's office, but I understood why Joe hadn't thought of them when he needed help. They didn't even have a proper police station out at the beach, just a little storefront office at Casino Beach, the main tourist area. The Chief was required to call them, since they had jurisdiction, but from his side of the conversation I had the impression he would remain in charge.

When he got off the phone he looked at Emily. "I understand you know this man?"

"A little. He and his wife, Karen, belong to the same activist group as me."

"Is there anyone you can call?"

Emily looked distressed. "They have two grown children, but I don't even know their names."

"We'll track them down. Is there anyone else you can think of to call now?"

"I guess I could call Laurel. She's in the group, too. It seems like they're friends."

"Do that."

While Emily made her call, The Chief put his phone away and tugged his belt up. "I'm headed out to the beach to see what's what," he said. He glanced over his shoulder at me as he left. "You lady detectives are welcome to join me if you like."

I looked at Mike hopefully. I desperately wanted to go. After a slight pause, he gave a tiny nod. I grabbed Emily and headed for the door, careful not to make eye contact with Rosario.

CHAPTER FOUR

A feeling of motion is what Karen was aware of first. It was making her headachy and more than a little nauseated, and she wanted it to stop. But she couldn't quite wake up enough to figure out how to make it do so. She got as far as that thought, "Make it stop," and then she drifted back into unconsciousness, which was a relief because it made her pounding head and the nausea fade away.

She went through several cycles of this, until the headache penetrated even to her unconscious. She was dreaming, and in her dream she and Joe were at home in their bedroom, only for some reason their queen-sized platform bed had been replaced by bunk beds. Joe told her she had to sleep on the top bunk. "All right," she said, though she felt a bit put out by this. She climbed up to the top bunk and lay down. But she had barely placed her head on the pillow when she felt a strong sense of vertigo, like the mattress was tipping underneath her. Then she fell to the floor, and her head exploded in pain.

"Ow!" she said. Then she woke up and realized she wasn't in her bedroom, and had no particular reason to be angry with Joe. Her head was killing her, though, and she was very cramped and uncomfortable. And she couldn't really move. And it was dark, except for a thin stream of sunlight trickling in from above her head.

Then she had it. She was in a car. She was in the goddamned trunk of a car, and her hands were tied behind her back, and her legs were tied, too, and her head was pounding as though last night had been a five-martini night, and she wanted to throw up.

She wasn't gagged, though, and the ropes around her hands didn't feel too tight. She supposed that was something.

The most important thing was not to panic. If you panicked, then the opposition had already won. Plus, one had to take whatever steps one could. She began squirming around until her feet were pointed toward one of the taillights. It was too bad she didn't have sneakers on rather than these stupid Tevas, but oh well. With one hard kangaroo thrust, she kicked out the driver's-side taillight.

CHAPTER FIVE

By the time Em and I pulled out of the office parking lot, The Chief and his cruiser were already out of sight. I followed at a more leisurely pace. From Shoreline I turned right onto McAbee Court. Emily looked at me quizzically.

"Shortcut," I explained. From McAbee you could cut through the Bahama Bay Condominiums parking lot, then turn directly onto the beach road without ever having to get on 98.

The water of the Santa Rosa Sound shimmered all around us as we sailed over the Bob Sikes Bridge. I slowed at the tollbooth, waving at the toll collector as the sensor scanned my bridge pass. I knew the tollbooth guy. A local musician named Josh, he'd been a few years behind me at Gulf Breeze High. He had fluffy blond dreadlocks that he kept tied back during his stints at the tollbooth, the day job that kept him supplied with reeds and mouthpieces (he was a sax player). He was clad in the bridge employees' uniform, which consisted of a flowered Hawaiian shirt and, in Josh's case, board shorts.

The Hawaiian-shirt-as-uniform was typical of what we residents of the Redneck Riviera like to call "the Salt Life." At its most literal, Salt Life was the brand name of a chain of clothing stores that originated out of Jacksonville Beach. They sold t-shirts and beanies and stickers, as well as practical items like rash guards for surfers. But on the panhandle, Salt Life had come to mean more than just a brand. It meant a reverence for the local beaches, with their emerald green water and sugar white sand. And, whether one's preferred method of achieving the Salt Life was through fishing, surfing, diving, boating, or just chilling on the beach with a beer, it meant a commitment to living slow, steady, and stress-free.

This was the other side of the coin of panhandle life, counterpoint to the kind of crazy life that could lead a code enforcement officer on a routine code violation visit to get a meat cleaver stuck in him.

Of course, the attack on Jim had occurred in mainland Pensacola, where the tensions of poverty and high unemployment made the Salt Life harder to achieve.

But whacking an old man on the head and kidnapping his wife—right on Pensacola Beach—when they were babysitting sea turtles? C'mon, man. That was definitely not Salt Life.

At the end of Pensacola Beach Road I veered to the left and headed east on Via de Luna Boulevard. We quickly passed through the resort's tourist hub, where The Dock and the Sandshaker and Peg Leg Pete's kept a constant stream of reggae and Jimmy Buffet pouring out into the open air through externally mounted loudspeakers, assuring tourists that the Salt Life was theirs for the purchasing. Next was a strip mall and the Circle K. The strip mall contained a Laundromat, a sandwich shop I could never remember the name of, the Native Café, and the Islander and Paddy O'Leary's—smaller bars that featured live music and catered to locals. After the strip mall there were a couple of older beach motels that hadn't yet been knocked down to make way for corporate chains. They were the kind of place young couples could afford to take their kids, where the carpet was threadbare and the furniture battered. But that just meant you didn't have to worry about tracking sand everywhere when you came back to the room, sunburned and tired, starving and happy, after staying on the beach all day.

After the drive-up motels Via de Luna passed abruptly into a residential area. The new and the old, the fancy and the shabby rubbed shoulders here. A large, South Florida–style mansion, frosted pink like an enormous birthday cake, might be on the lot right next to a cinderblock shack. Shabby or fancy, though, all the houses shared the same golden status of being less than 100 yards from the Gulf.

"Someday," I said, as I always did when I drove through this neighborhood. Meaning, somehow, someday, I'll have a place out here too. Hurricanes be damned.

"Someday," Emily agreed.

We passed the famous UFO house, which had been a Pensacola Beach landmark my whole life. It was actually a Futuro—a type of Jetsons-ish, prefab house designed by a Finnish company in the late '60s and early '70s. The Futuro is a disk-shaped, fiberglass building that resembles a flying saucer. When I was a girl, Keith used to take me there on Halloween, when the owners would drape the saucer with orange sailcloth and turn it into a giant jack-o-lantern.

After the UFO house there were a few more blocks of single-family residences, and then the condos started, culminating in Portofino. Portofino was a giant, multi-tower condominium complex, built in 2004—just in time for Hurricane Ivan. It had been a dividing point in the community when it was first proposed in 2003. The environmentalists had been up in arms, protesting the loss of wetlands and questioning the need for so many new high-end condos in our small community. When the County Commission, bolstered by the Chamber of Commerce and the local Builders' Association, pushed it through anyway, only to see the first tower promptly damaged by Ivan, the tree-huggers seemed vindicated. Then, for a while, with housing at a premium after Ivan and Dennis and everyone flush with insurance money, the developers had seemed to score a victory, as it looked like real estate would continue to expand, unabated, forever. But when the housing bubble popped in 2007 it popped at Portofino just like everywhere else. Now many of the condos sat vacant. Some had been foreclosed on; others had never been inhabited in the first place.

We drove half a mile past the main cluster of Portofino buildings until we got to Tower Three, which was the easternmost portion of the development. Set off from the others, it sat right on the edge of a segment of the Gulf Islands National Seashore, offering its mostly hypothetical residents glorious views of pristine, federally protected beach.

"What do you think—should I park at the Tower?"

"No, keep going. Here it is," Em said as we reached a public parking lot a short distance beyond the condos.

"And there's The Chief," I said, spotting his cruiser.

I parked next to The Chief and we climbed out of the truck. This wasn't a surfing beach, and it was still too early for regular beachgoers, so the lot was mostly empty—there was an RV parked at the far east end, but aside from that it was my truck, The Chief's cruiser, a couple of patrol cars from the Beach Patrol, and an SUV from the Pensacola Police Department's Criminal Investigations Division—the crime scene unit. I was impressed they'd gotten here so quickly. They must have flown over the Three Mile Bridge.

I could see a couple of uniforms roping off a section of the beach with stakes and crime tape. Inside the tape, two crime scene techs knelt in the sand, taking casts of footprints. Within the tape barrier I could also see a large area of disturbed sand. I recognized it as a post-boil sea turtle nest.

The Chief was strolling around outside the perimeter of the tape, staring intently down at the sand. There was someone else with him, a younger man in a collared shirt and tie I didn't recognize.

When he spotted us, The Chief straightened up and headed over, wiping his brow. The temperature was already pushing 90 degrees.

"What's happening?" I asked when he got close enough.

"It's a mess. I was hoping your friend was mistaken," he added, glancing at Emily, "and that maybe he and his wife were just victims of a robbery. But we've looked all over, and I sent a car to their house, too. No sign of her. It seems like she really was snatched."

"What do you think they wanted with Karen?"

"Money," The Chief said promptly. "That's what they always want. We need to get Joe set up for the ransom call."

"But he and Karen aren't rich!" Emily protested. "I mean, I think they're comfortable, but why on earth would they be targeted for money, with all the rich folks and their beach homes and giant sailing yachts around here?"

"Most kidnapping victims aren't extremely rich," The Chief said. "What matters is that their families can get their hands on cash quickly. The kidnappers must have gotten the impression Joe has access to a fair amount of it."

"So it's someone who knows him?" I asked.

"Possibly. Someone who has access to knowledge about him, anyway."

"You said kidnappers, plural. You think there's more than one?"

"There usually is. So far we've only been able to find one set of footprints, but the partner may have been waiting at the car. You want to come out and take a look?"

We followed The Chief onto the beach. The guy with the tie walked over to join us. "Gail, Emily, this is Detective Jeffers from the sheriff's office," The Chief said.

"Are you ladies with the force?" Jeffers asked.

"Special Task Force: Planning & Zoning," I said.

Jeffers didn't crack a smile. "I didn't think this was a zoning matter," he said, turning to The Chief.

"We believe it's tied to some signs that were illegally placed in Gulf Breeze," Emily said, a tad snappishly. She disliked it when people didn't warm to me. It was cute. But I thought it might be a mistake to mention the signs to Jeffers. It would complicate things unnecessarily.

"There's probably no connection," I said quickly. "We've been having the sign problem for some time. But there was something a little different about one of the signs we found today, and we just wanted to make sure it wasn't related. I'm Gail LaRue," I added, sticking my hand straight out at Jeffers.

He flinched at the prospect of touching me. I was used to this reaction. Actually, a lot of men who catch sight of my 5' 10" frame and platinum blonde hair and The Girls do want to touch me, kind of a lot. But the buttoned-up type like Jeffers is another story.

He looked down at my hand like it might give him cooties, then reluctantly reached out and touched my fingertips.

I grabbed his fingers and crushed them a little. Then I dropped them and strode past him toward the crime scene tape. Emily scurried behind me. I walked right up to the tape and stopped. The technicians were hunched over their drying casts, their backs to Em and me.

"How's it going?" I called.

The techs turned, startled. But then they smiled.

"Pretty good," the nearer one said, grinning up at me. He was probably in his late 20s, with black-rimmed glasses, stringy black hair falling into his eyes, and a bit of a belly discernible beneath his voluminous golf shirt. Despite the blinding sunshine, he'd made no effort—a tinted prescription, a pair of clip-ons—to shield his eyes from the sun. A tech geek through and through.

"Whaddaya got?" I asked him.

"Looks like the snatcher was a male wearing size nine athletic shoes. He walks with a limp. Favors the left side. We've also accounted for the victim and her husband."

"Wearing his and hers Tevas, sizes nine and a half and six, respectively," the second tech chimed in. He was smaller than the first guy, with brown skin, black hair, and nicely muscled arms. I placed him in his early 20s.

"That sounds about right," Emily said. "They're sort of hippies."

"We figured," said the first guy. "Not that there's anything wrong with that," he added. "It's nice what they do for the turtles."

The second guy snorted, but said nothing.

"You have a problem with that?" I asked him.

"Not the turtle stuff," the guy said. "But they're the same people who are always trying to stop development. It's bogus."

I glanced Emily's way to see how she would respond. This was the kind of thing that usually got her blood boiling. But Em wasn't paying attention. She was staring past the techs over to the far side of the cordoned-off rea.

"What is it?"

"I'm not sure." She started walking around the crime scene tape. I followed. We walked 180 degrees, until we were directly opposite the place where we'd been standing a moment before. Then Emily veered away from the tape to the east a little bit. She bent and picked something up.

"What did you find?"

"A turtle shell."

"Well, yeah, they're everywhere. A nest just hatched."

Emily clutched the shell fragment. She looked around for a bit, then started up the beach toward a gap between two dunes that led to the road. She bent again.

"Another shell?"

"Yeah."

"You thinking Hansel and Gretel?"

Em nodded.

I followed with more interest now. She bent twice more before we reached the road, collecting the shell fragments on her palm. At the road she found another, then after looking around for a moment she started walking along the road, continuing east. But then she stopped. "Oh oh."

"What's the matter?"

Emily pointed into the sand on the shoulder of the road. I followed her arm and looked down. The crushed remnants of a turtle shell lay scattered in the sand. "Looks like someone stole her breadcrumbs."

Back at the office, Rosario silently handed Emily and I each a new stack of post-it notes. I slunk back to my office with mine and was shuffling through the pile, looking for the least obnoxious possibility, when Emily came in and plopped herself down in the visitor's chair.

"Do you think I should call Joe?"

"Yes."

"I know I should."

"Well, what's stopping you?"

"I'm chicken."

"Here, give me your phone. I'll call him."

"Maybe I should call Laurel instead. In case he's too upset to talk."

"Fine. Call Laurel."

"Okay." She set her head down on my desk, puffed out her cheeks, and exhaled, scattering my post-it notes.

"You're not calling."

"I know."

"I have an idea. Let's just go over there."

"Okay. But maybe we should let Rosario take her lunch first. I don't think she's thrilled with how much we've been out of the office. Anyway, she goes early—she should be back by noon."

"You're leaving me with no choice but to call these angry, code-violating residents."

"Work your magic," Em said, returning to the outer office.

When she stuck her head in my office an hour later and asked, "Ready?" I'm ashamed to report that I still had not returned the calls of Mr. Angelo, who was calling (as he did every week) to complain that the builders working on the lot next to his were leaving dirt in the street; or of Ms. Packer, who was calling (as she did once a month) to complain about the unsightly POD (a type of portable storage unit) her neighbors had planted in their backyard. And I certainly hadn't called anyone from Yellow Tree.

Instead, I had passed the time Photoshopping the picture of Jackie Willis wielding her bread knife. First, I'd added myself into the picture. I'd put myself off to the side, in a Charlie's Angels martial arts pose (I'd used my head from one of our wedding pics and borrowed Cameron Diaz's body from the Internet). I'd given myself a speaking part; a speech bubble over my head said, "Drop the bread knife, Willis!"

Next, I'd added a giant loaf of bread. It was floating in the air in front of Jackie, so it appeared she was about to slice the loaf in half with a big old Samurai swing.

Finally, I'd posted a title across the top of the picture: "The Greatest Thing Since Sliced Bread."

Okay, so it wasn't my most mature moment. But between Jackie and Karen and Joe, it had been an unusually stressful morning. Plus, I'm not crazy about hospitals. I thought Em and I should go, but that didn't mean I was looking forward to it.

When we got to the hospital we stopped in the gift shop for

flowers before heading up in the elevator. Joe was on the fourth floor. We ran into Laurel, Emily's friend from PFC, sitting in the fourth-floor lounge. Laurel was in her late 60s, same as Joe, and had a similar hippie vibe about her. She had shoulder-length white hair and was wearing a tie-dyed skirt that fell to the floor and a t-shirt with a rainbow on it. She stood and hugged Emily.

"How's he doing?"

"He's resting now. They gave him a sedative."

"They're not worried about a concussion?"

"They did a brain scan. They're still waiting on the results but the doctor who examined him seemed to think he'll be okay. He was more worried about Joe's emotional state. He was frantic about Karen."

"Chief Tobin thought he would be contacted about a ransom."

Laurel looked startled. "I don't think he's heard from anyone."

We headed down the corridor. It was easy to tell which room was Joe's because The Chief himself stood in front of the door, impassive, arms across his chest. He greeted us quietly. Peeking around him, I saw Joe dozing in the nearer of two hospital beds. His head was propped up and wrapped with a bandage. The second bed was unoccupied. Over by the window, a police tech hunched in a chair, scooched up close to one of those rolling dinner carts. He was using it as a makeshift desk and had a bunch of electronics equipment arrayed in front of him.

Emily tiptoed into the room and set the flowers on the dresser beside Joe's bed. She touched his forehead and looked at the displays on the medical equipment, then took a seat in an empty chair and held his hand.

"Em's friend said there hasn't been a ransom call," I murmured to The Chief.

"No." He looked troubled. "I'm hoping it comes in soon. If

we don't get a ransom call, that means someone wanted Karen for something other than money."

CHAPTER SIX

The only result of kicking out the taillight was that Karen lost one of her Tevas. When she got her feet out through the hole she wiggled them around a little, figuring this might get the attention of the driver behind them. But she must have wiggled too much, because suddenly the left sandal, whose heel strap had slipped off the back of her foot during the kick, started to fall off.

"No!" she cried, turning the foot up, trying to catch the sandal. But she was too late. It slid off and slapped against the pavement below.

Surely some other driver saw *that*? But no one came to the rescue. Now that she thought about it, Karen wasn't sure she could hear any other cars on the road at all. Where the hell were they? Someplace rural, it had to be. Maybe up toward Milton, in northern Santa Rosa County? That would mean they'd crossed a bridge—two of them, in fact, if you counted the one from the barrier island to the peninsula. She had no memory of crossing any bridges. They must have done so while she was still knocked out.

She could feel herself starting to tear up, lamenting the loss of the sandal, which seemed to make her even more vulnerable. Plus her head was still pounding.

"None of that now," she muttered to herself. "Get a grip." She knew she needed to keep her head clear, not give in to fear.

The car slowed almost to a stop, then made a right turn. The new road was uneven, and she could feel gravel splaying up onto her feet. A dirt road. They *were* in the country. The driver drove fast, swerving now and then as though to avoid the worst of the bumps and ditches. He knew the road.

The bouncing was a little nauseating. Karen drew her feet back into the trunk. No use leaving them exposed out there if they were on a deserted dirt road with no one to see them.

After a fairly long drive down the dirt road—maybe half a mile, Karen estimated, which doesn't sound long but feels like 10 times that when it's all ruts and bumps and you're in a *trunk*—the car slowed to a stop and the driver parked. She felt a kernel of fear sprouting in her stomach and tried to change it to anger. How dare someone stick her in a trunk? It was an awful, smelly, sickening place.

She curled herself into the fetal position with her legs curled above her. There was a pause after the engine was cut, then she heard the driver's-side door open and shut. Another pause and she heard the key in the trunk. She braced herself. When the trunk lid opened, the brightness blinded her, but she was able to see the outline of her captor. He didn't look that big.

She figured out where his face was and kicked right below that, with all her might. He went down. She swung her legs over the edge of the trunk and sat up. The rope around her legs had loosened. She pushed it off with her hands still tied and started running toward the road.

But her kidnapper quickly regained his breath and his feet.

CHAPTER SEVEN

We stopped at Whataburger on the way back to the office.

"I hate to think of some creep messing with Karen," Em said as I steered the truck around the building.

"I know. But you said she's a pretty tough cookie, right? Hopefully she can hold her own until they find her."

"They have so little to go on, though. Not even a description of the car. Just a limp and a size 9 shoe."

"Here, have an onion ring," I said, shoving one into Em's mouth. "You need to keep your strength up. I know it's scary, but I have a good feeling about Karen."

Back at the office Rosario handed us our post-it notes. I only had three, and they were all repeat customers—Mr. Angelo, Ms. Packer, and Mr. Crable from Yellow Tree. I considered this a victory.

As I rounded the corner into my office, I was startled to see someone waiting there. It was Shawn O'Brien, aka the sign guy. He was slouched in the guest chair, staring vacantly across the desk at the empty space where I would normally be sitting.

Emily must be right; Rosario must be super pissed at us. Otherwise, there's no way she would have let me walk into a room with Shawn in it without giving me a warning. He wasn't popular around the office anyway, but Rosario in particular loathed him. Normally she'd give me a head's-up if he were around, even try to prevent him from entering my office al-together.

From the outer office, I heard laughing. I suppose I deserved it from Rosario, but Emily was laughing, too, the traitor.

"Hey, Shawn, what's up?" I said grumpily, giving him a wide berth as I skirted around his chair and took my seat behind the desk.

"They're at it again."

"I know. I picked up five on the way in." I left out the part about two of them being copycats. I didn't have the energy to hear Shawn's theories about the new signs.

"Five? Wow." Just for a moment, he looked surprised. Then he turned vacant again. "I have an idea for how to catch them."

"Pray tell."

"I'll need your help." He was silent at this point, and so was I. It was always like this, talking to Shawn. Was I supposed to beg to hear his idea? Yes, I suspected I was supposed to beg. Well, good luck with that.

Seeing that no begging was forthcoming, he finally spoke up again. "Though the placement of the signs changes a lot, I've noticed lately there's always one near the entrance to the Cost-mart. So, we just need to set up a surveillance trap there. At night, of course, since it seems pretty clear that's when they put them out. Do you think Mike would approve us for some overtime for a stakeout?"

Us? A stakeout? I pictured being stuck in my pickup, with Shawn, in the Costmart parking lot, all night long, listening as he described soaping his wife's back.

The picture filled me with despair, so maybe I spoke a little more sharply than I should have. "I don't know. I guess I could ask him. What I do know is you're not really staying on top of the problem the way we hoped when we hired you."

He looked affronted. "I'm doing my best. I'm just one man, and I'm only authorized to work part time."

Already I felt remorseful. "I didn't mean it like that."

"No, it's okay. I'd rather you talked to me frankly." I had the horrible suspicion he might cry. "I guess I'd better get out there, then. I didn't know my job performance left something to be desired."

"It's not like that, Shawn. Wait . . ." But he'd already risen from his chair and was backing out of the office, his eyes blinking rapidly.

"See you," he said in a choking voice and disappeared.

For about three seconds, I contemplated going after him, but then I decided against it. I was sorry I'd hurt his feelings, but the idea that maybe he would skip the long pointless updates in my office for a while was too tempting to mess with.

I was reshuffling my post-it notes yet again when someone burst into my office. I was afraid Shawn had returned to cry on my blotter, but when I looked up it was Mike who stood in front of my desk.

Mike was in his early 40s. He had thick wavy black hair that he controlled with some sort of hair oil, and deep-set brown eyes. He was handsome but a little out of shape. He adored his wife and two kids but didn't see them much during the week. His devotion to Community Development was fanatical. Basically he was working himself to death.

"I see you made Shawn cry."

"Oh crap, was he really?"

Mike laughed. "It's okay by me. But listen, he may be an idiot, but he's right about one thing. We need to step it up, in terms of catching those GulfBreezeSingles guys. It seems like the letter didn't work out."

"No, I guess not," I said, stifling my "I told you so." After all, I hadn't ever told him so, except in my head. "What did you have in mind?"

"Don't laugh, but I was thinking *we* should make some signs."

"What kind of signs?"

"Signs offering a reward for information about the people putting out the other signs."

Here it was. Captain Ahab had gone off the deep end. "We can't do that."

"Why not?"

"We'll be breaking the sign ordinance, for one thing."

"I already talked to Richard." Richard was Chair of the Planning Commission. "He said the Commission will approve the signs for us."

"It doesn't matter whether they do or not. In fact, if they do, that will only make it worse. If we put signs out, every busybody in Gulf Breeze with too much time on his hands will be calling me about it. And everybody we've ever cited for violating the sign ordinance will be calling and threatening to sue because we made an exception for ourselves but not for them."

Fortunately, even from the depths of obsession, Mike's sense of fair play, and fear of bad precedent-setting, could always be counted upon. His face fell. "I guess you're right. But we have to do something!"

Those signs were eating him alive. "Why don't you put something on the website? Everything you were planning to put on the sign, put it on a web page. The message should be, We need your help. Make people feel like they're solving a mystery. Vigilante justice. People love that. We'll have our sign guy by the end of the week."

"I guess I could do that." A spark of hope had reignited in Mike's eye. "I'll get started on it right away. I'll let you know when I have something worked up so you can take a look."

Mike returned to his office, leaving me with my little stack of While You Were Out notes again. It was proving to be the longest afternoon in the history of office work. I set the pile down and went out to the front counter to see what Emily was up to.

Finally, the workday drew to a close. Right before five o'clock,

The Chief stopped by to give us an update. The doctors said Joe was going to be okay. Police had canvassed everyone in Portofino Tower Three—no one had seen anything that might be useful. They didn't even have a make and model for the kidnapper's car. There'd been no ransom call.

"What about the RV we saw parked in the beach lot?" Emily asked.

"We checked. It's a retired couple—they've been traveling around in that thing for the past two years. Kind of cool, actually. But they slept in until eight o'clock, so they missed whatever happened with Karen and Joe. Also, Gail, the Park Service ordered a necropsy on that turtle of yours. They want to make sure the kidnapper didn't do something twisted."

We all contemplated this in silence for a moment. "What now?" asked Mike, who'd joined us at the front counter.

"We're going to the media. I'm doing a live interview with WEAR at six o'clock."

"What are you going to say?"

"We're going to tell the community what happened. Ask if anyone saw anything. Ask for their help."

I caught Mike's eye and nodded knowingly.

On the drive home I stopped to pick up subs. When I turned onto our street there was Chris, shooting hoops with some of the kids from the neighborhood.

Chris and I had been married for a little over a year. We'd been friends since our first week at FSU, but didn't start dating until we were juniors.

I pledged Kappa Kappa Gamma my freshman year, as did most of the FSU softball players. There were many things I loved about KKG. One of the things I loved was that KKG was technically not a sorority but a women's fraternity. (It was founded before the word *sorority* had been invented.) I also loved the fact that Kate Jackson, Kate Spade, and Mariska Hargitay were all Kappas. Most of all, I loved hanging out with my sisters (or my brothers, as we jokingly liked to refer to each other).

However, despite the fact that we were our own fraternity, at FSU we did partner with a particular men's fraternity, Alpha Tau Omega, for our service and social events.

We partied with them, in other words. Chris pledged ATO at the same time I pledged KKG. Like me, he was an athlete. He played point guard on the men's basketball team and was good enough that he made the starting team during our junior year. In the spring he played lacrosse. He could easily have been a starting outfielder for the baseball team, but he loved lacrosse too much to give it up, even though the lacrosse team at FSU was non-NCAA.

We met during pledge week, hit it off immediately, and remained good buds for the next two years. Chris dated all of my friends, and I dated all of his. Whenever one of us had a particularly bad date, or a painful breakup, we'd call the other and meet up for a beer. We'd laugh immediately about the bad dates, and eventually we could always turn the breakups into a funny story, too.

Then, on Halloween during out junior year, I had a date that went south before we'd even made it out of Kappa house. It was my fault. I'd just started taking a new birth control pill and it was making me crazy. I'm not normally much of a weeper, but that pill had me crying like a church on Monday. My hormones were in overdrive. On the night in question, first I got upset about how I looked in my costume (zombie cheerleader). Then I changed about 17 times, burst into tears, wiped off all my makeup, and put my bathrobe back on. That was where things stood when my date, a dude named Dan, arrived to pick me up.

I was sitting on the couch, sniffling, when one of my house-mates let him in. He asked why I wasn't ready. This was a perfectly reasonable question. For one thing, he was already running a little late, so I'd had extra time to get ready. More to the point, for a girly girl I prided myself on being able to get up and go quickly, with a minimum of primping, and this fact was well known in our circle.

But despite the reasonableness of Dan's question, I had a complete, come-to-Jesus meltdown and let him have a big old dose of hormones with both barrels.

Ten minutes later, Dan fled Kappa house in terror. Still cry-ing, I called Chris. He was already at the party, but said he'd be right over. I managed to get out of my bathrobe and into a pair of shorts and a t-shirt before he arrived, so I wasn't too *When Harry Met Sally* by the time he got there, but overall I was still in pretty lame shape.

Five minutes later he had me laughing hysterically at my own behavior. I put on my costume and we reenacted me chasing poor Dan out of the house, only this time with me as a zombie cheerleader. Then Chris suggested I might want to think about going back to my old birth control method.

At that point it hadn't occurred to me yet that the pills were the problem creating my sudden and calamitous emotional imbalance. I considered this a stunning insight and went over to give him a friendly little thank-you kiss.

The next thing I knew, we were making out.

Chris grew up in Clearwater, Florida, in a family with parents who were happily married and a younger brother and sister he adored and who worshipped him. He majored in early child-hood education, with a minor in sports management. He always knew he wanted to be a teacher. But when I was applying for planning jobs during our senior year, he said I should take whatever job I wanted the most because he could find a teach-

69

ing job anywhere.

I received offers from a few mid-sized cities around the South—Knoxville, Tuscaloosa, Wilmington. But then I got the call from Mike. I'd sent the application to Gulf Breeze on a whim—they weren't even advertising a job opening. But once I got the offer, I couldn't stop thinking about coming home, even though by then I wasn't even really sure I could call Gulf Breeze home anymore. I no longer had family in the area, or any other ties to the place except my memories. Still, I realized I wanted to take the job.

"No problem," Chris said when I told him I wanted to come here. Even when I pointed out that our career advancement would probably be much slower here than in one of those other cities, that's what he said. I gave him every chance to talk me out of it, but he just kept repeating it. "No problem. Whatever you want."

So we came to Gulf Breeze. Bought a ramshackle little house on a canal that leads out to Pensacola Bay. Got married. And just as he'd predicted, Chris found a job easily. He teaches sixth-grade science at Gulf Breeze Middle School, as well as coaching little league baseball and basketball there.

The neighborhood kids worship him. He's just a big kid himself. A giant kid, actually. He's 6' 6" and wide as a barn, with cowlicky, sandy blond hair.

When I climbed out of the car, he grinned and stole the ball from the kid who was trying to dribble it, then ran over and gave me a kiss. The little boys watched bashfully.

"Aren't you going to say hello to my wife?" he teased them.

"Hey, Mrs. L.," they mumbled.

"Hey, boys. Anybody want subs?" I'd picked up a few extra.

"Okay!"

"Go ask your parents."

While they ran off to get permission, Chris hustled me into

the house. "You're the best! I'm starving!"

I'd been planning on giving him hell for buying an Evo 4G that day without consulting me first. I'd logged onto our bank account before I left the office and saw the charge. The man was addicted to cell phones, and he spent his schoolteacher's wages like a CEO. But now that I was home, it didn't seem worth the bother.

CHAPTER EIGHT

Karen regained consciousness to absolute, searing pain in her head. She'd thought her head ached before; now she realized the earlier pain had just been a frolic. Play pain. A rehearsal for this.

"Oww," she said, dragging her eyes open and looking around.

She was indoors, in an unfamiliar room. It was lit by two smoked glass table lamps. They were kind of fabulous, but the rest of the room didn't do them justice. It was a lot of mismatched cheap wooden furniture, some dusty deer heads mounted on the wall, and the telltale sign of a maniac that we've all learned from TV: a wall covered with newspaper clippings, some of them marked up with angry-looking magic marker. Karen herself was lying face down on a musty calico couch.

"You're up then," an unfamiliar voice said. Southern born and bred. A deep drawl. Older.

Karen took stock of herself. Her aching arms were still tied behind her back and her legs had been retied. She raised her head and sought out the voice.

"Easy now." She had to turn her head—ouch—to find him. He was sitting in a rocker to her right, on the other side of a trunk that served as a coffee table. Karen put him at about Joe's age—late 60s, maybe five years older than Karen herself, though his skin was so sun damaged it was hard to tell for sure. He was skinny and wore a flannel shirt with work pants and boots. He had a gun pointed at her.

"I've had to hit you twice in the head now. I don't want to hit you again. I need your head."

Karen was taking deep, slow breaths, trying to manage the pain and stay calm, but at these words she felt her hair stand straight up. Who the hell was this guy? A serial killer who— collected heads?

"Are you hungry?"

"No."

"You should eat something. And drink. You don't want to get dehydrated. Here." He lifted a tray from the end table next to him and set it on the trunk. It held a bowl of soup, a roll, and a mug of tea, as well as a folded napkin with a spoon and a butter knife placed daintily on top. The soup appeared to be a tomato-based vegetable, and there was hummus to go with the bread, rather than butter—as though he knew she was vegan. The soup smelled good. Karen felt her stomach rumble and realized she *was* hungry.

"I can't eat with my hands tied."

"I know. I'm going to untie you. No funny business, though, right?"

"Whatever you say." The man came close and untied the rope around her arms. Karen tried to hide the revulsion she experienced when she felt him touch her. He smelled musty, like the couch. She switched to shallow breaths through the mouth.

When he stepped away and went back to his chair, Karen moved to an upright position and returned to her deep breathing, willing herself to stay calm. It was actually hard to panic, though, with her head pounding so hard it made her dizzy. For a moment she thought she might faint.

"My head is killing me."

"I'll get you some aspirins. I don't think you should take

anything stronger. You might be concussed."

He rose and shuffled out of the room. He walked with a limp, favoring his left side.

Watching him leave, Karen realized this was her moment to act. She might not get another chance. She'd been left alone, she had a butter knife—she might never have a better opportunity than this.

She had always believed fighting was the right answer for women who were attacked or abducted. Fight, struggle, yell, resist. And yet . . . and yet right now she just wanted to eat her damn soup. She didn't even care if it was poisoned. Her head hurt so bad it was torture to think of standing up, let alone running.

She wanted her head to stop pounding, and she wanted to eat.

So, she gave herself permission to do so. She forgave herself for settling for food and tea and aspirin, for comfort rather than freedom, and made a vow that she wouldn't hold this moment against herself later, no matter what happened next.

CHAPTER NINE

The next morning I arrived at work with a renewed sense of purpose. Over breakfast I'd decided I would start the work day by making all the phone calls I'd skipped over yesterday. Then I'd go out and do a round of site visits regarding code violation complaints, then head straight back to the office and write letters. My slacker days were over.

I'd also decided I was going to mind my own beeswax regarding Karen and Joe. It was sad, but it was really none of my business. I was sure The Chief had things well in hand.

Finally, I'd decided I was going to run over to Pensacola on my lunch hour to get Rosario a package of pralines from Renfroe's. Rosario loved pralines, and only Renfroe's would do. It had been foolish to incur Rosario's wrath. I needed to make amends.

When I walked into the office Emily and Rosario were both on the phone. They both rolled their eyes at me rather desperately as I passed. What the hell? I slowed to listen to Em's call.

"Thank you for the information. As I mentioned, you should probably call the Tip Line, but I'll let The Chief know as well."

"Wtf, Mate?" I mouthed. Em shook her head wearily.

I was curious, but I didn't want my willpower to be derailed by curiosity, so I continued back to my office. As I settled at my desk and turned the computer on, I heard Emily wrap up her call and hang up. Almost immediately, her phone rang again. In a moment, she was saying, "We really appreciate you calling, but you'll want to call the Tip Line . . ." before being cut off again. Even when she added, rather desperately, "You won't be eligible for the reward unless you call the Tip Line," she couldn't shake the caller.

So that was it. The Chief must have announced a Tip Hotline during his TV appearance last night, but some of the Breezers were calling the city directly instead. I had meant to watch him on the news, but then when I got home I got all caught up with Chris and the neighbor kids and I forgot.

Evidently someone had posted a reward. It must have been Joe, right? The Chief had probably suggested the idea to him.

I was tempted to go back out to the outer office and stop Emily before she took another call, so I could find out if my guesses were correct. But if I did so, I was afraid that would be it for making my own calls. Therefore I resisted temptation and stayed planted in my chair.

Before picking up the handset, though, I braced myself. I had a feeling that, in addition to the usual complaints about weeds and dirt, this morning I was going to be treated to some kidnapping theories.

Sure enough, once I had him on the phone, Mr. Angelo observed that it was a terrible thing what had happened to Karen Baretta, but you couldn't expect to be a rabble-rousing troublemaker and have a quiet life. This was, I assumed, a reference to Karen's environmental activism. Twenty minutes later, Ms. Packer expressed doubts that all was well in the Baretta household.

I made note of these theories for future discussion with Emily. An hour later I'd finally worked through my messages. Setting the handset down in its cradle, I looked at the phone's light board. It appeared Emily and Rosario had cleared their calls as well.

Just then Emily's face appeared in my doorway. She looked a little wild-eyed. When I waved her in, she collapsed into the visitor's chair.

"Why do they think we're the Tip Line?" she wailed.

"They've got us on speed dial. It's easier than learning a new phone number."

"I called The Chief to ask what we should do. He said as long as we make it clear to them that we're not the Tip Line, and that they're not eligible for the reward unless they call the Tip Line, he wants us to keep taking the calls. I guess they're swamped over there, too. He said he trusts us to make note of anything interesting."

"Speaking of which . . ." I told her about the theories from Mr. Angelo and Ms. Packer.

Emily looked startled at the suggestion that all was not well between Karen and Joe. "But he got bonked on the head, too."

"Well, that's how they do it, right, if they want to deflect suspicion away from themselves? The spouse or lover, I mean. Get the hitman to shoot them in the knee or something."

"I guess," Em said. She looked glum. "But the spouse is always a suspect anyway, right? So The Chief is probably exploring that angle already. I'm not saying you shouldn't pass it on to him. I'm just saying I don't want to think about it."

"Who put up the reward?"

"Joe. And Panhandlers for Change added some, too."

"That's nice of you."

"It's just a gesture, really—a little bit on top of Joe's amount. Andy called us all last night to see if we wanted to do it, and we all agreed."

Glancing at the phone, I noticed that Rosario was on a call again and Emily's line was ringing. "I guess we'd better get back to it."

"Yeah. Can you do lunch? I was reading more about the

mitigation banks last night, and I'd like to talk it out."

"You bet." So much for minding my own business.

Rosario took her lunch first. When I heard her return, I headed out to the front office. "Ready?"

"Yeah," Emily said. Miraculously, she was off the phone for the moment. As soon as Rosario's butt touched her chair we scurried out of the office before the guilt of leaving her alone with the Tip Line callers overwhelmed us.

"Any more interesting tips?" I asked as we climbed into my truck.

"A few more people put forward the 'Husband Who Hired a Hit Man' theory."

"That's just what people always think. I'm sure it doesn't mean anything. Where should we go?"

"I don't really feel like fast food."

"Me neither. Let's go to the Car Wash."

The best Thai place on the panhandle, and one of my all-time favorite restaurants, was a combination Thai lunch buffet and car wash located in north Pensacola. The buffet included California rolls and spring rolls, lemongrass soup and coconut milk soup, three kinds of curry, Pad Thai, and a whole host of other yummies, all emptied and replenished constantly so they never acquired that lukewarm, soggy buffet food feel and taste.

Plus, if you sat in one of the booths on the north wall, you could watch cars go through the automated car wash while you ate your Pad Thai. For some reason I found this extremely entertaining.

At the restaurant we loaded up our trays, then took a seat at one of the booths with a car wash view. Emily sipped her Thai iced tea, then took a bite of donut.

"Starting with dessert?" I teased.

"Technically, they're not dessert—as you know perfectly well." The donuts were found on the large buffet table that held entrees, not the smaller one covered with slices of pie and cups of pudding. Therefore Emily always maintained they weren't a dessert. "Besides, they're at the height of their deliciousness warm. Why let it get cold, just for the sake of convention?"

She took another bite of donut, then took her phone out of her purse, fiddled with the screen for a minute, and handed it to me.

There was a web page displayed. Scanning, I saw that it was minutes from a Panhandlers for Change meeting several weeks earlier. I looked at Emily quizzically.

"Read agenda item 3."

Agenda item 3 was long. It was about a proposed commercial development of 19 acres of wetlands at Eglin, the Air Force base 30 miles east of Gulf Breeze. The PFC group was concerned that the Air Force hadn't offered the land to the National Park Service before leasing it to a private developer. According to the notes, there was a clause in Eglin's development guidelines specifying that whenever the Air Force decided it didn't need land on the base, the Park Service was supposed to have first dibs. (I thought I detected the hand of Congressman Bob Sikes in such a clause: using one of his pet projects to feed another.) The purpose of offering the land to the Park Service was so it would have the chance to expand the Gulf Islands National Seashore. Since land in the National Seashore wasn't all contiguous to begin with, it didn't matter if new parcels didn't adjoin an existing section of the park.

In the case of the Eglin parcel, however, the Park Service had been bypassed altogether and the lease had been offered to a contractor who, according to the minutes, had been eyeing the property for the past 15 years.

The last paragraph might have been the most interesting. It said the developer, Chip Brown, planned to offset development of the wetlands by purchasing 19 acres in a mitigation bank located in northern Santa Rosa County.

"You guys talked about mitigation banks."

"Yup. And Karen hated them. Said it wasn't okay to destroy an ecosystem, and the idea of replicating it elsewhere was a crock. She compared the idea to losing a child, and someone brings you another 3-year-old girl with blue eyes and brown hair and says, 'Won't this one do just as well'?"

"Ouch. Probably best you didn't include that in the minutes." Emily served as recorder for the group.

"It sounds harsh, I know. But it was how she felt."

"So you think her disappearance has something to do with this?"

"I don't know. But doesn't it seem awfully strange that the sign about mitigation banks appeared at the Visitors' Center on the same day Karen disappeared? As you see, we publish our minutes on the Internet, so anyone could have read them. Including the kidnapper. Anyway, it seems like a much better lead than thinking Joe may have hurt her in some way. I know statistically it's likely to be the husband," Emily added quickly. "But I've seen them together. Joe dotes on Karen."

"What exactly is a mitigation bank?"

Emily looked surprised. "Didn't you study them at planner school?"

I was embarrassed and a touch annoyed. "It rings a bell, but why don't you fill me in anyway."

"Well, as I'm sure you know, the federal government passed the Clean Water Act in 1995. One of its stipulations is that developers who build on wetlands are now required to reclaim an acre of land for every acre of wetlands they fill in. The idea is it's supposed to be a zero-sum game where wetland acreage never gets smaller. But it can be hard for developers to find land they can reclaim, and of course most developers don't want to bother. They're interested in development, not in undevelopment, which is sort of what reclamation turns out to be. So developers starting looking around for other solutions.

"As far back as the '80s, Fish and Wildlife had supported the formation of 'wetland reclamation banks.' These were sites that were identified as good candidates for reclamation, so protected wetlands acreage could be consolidated. In the mid-'90s, the Feds let developers put these two ideas together, and designated wetlands mitigation banks started opening for business. Developers can pay a recognized mitigation bank to reclaim a piece of land equal in size to the acreage they're developing. The idea is that everyone stays on his own expertise. The developers develop, and the mitigation banks reclaim and maintain wetlands."

"A reasonable substitute. Kind of like when John Rockefeller hired some poor guy to go to war in his place during the Civil War draft." The analogy had come out of nowhere. Looks like I remembered Mr. Cole's American History lessons better than I thought. "Huh. I guess I'm making the same kind of comparison as Karen."

"Exactly. Her first objection was similar to what would happen in your analogy if the poor guy goes off and gets himself killed in battle. Then he's dead, and there's no swapping him back. She said even if you could create new wetlands elsewhere, that wasn't an excuse for killing off the old ones."

"If?"

"Yes, if. Her second objection was that it doesn't work. Evidently environmental scientists have gone to some of these sites and checked them out. It's not very easy to make land back into wetlands once it's been drained. Some of the land where reclamation was supposedly taking place was nice green space—but it was uplands, not wetlands."

"It sounds like Karen's opinions are right in line with the nutjob's website."

Her mouth full of spring roll, Emily nodded.

"So why would he kidnap her, if they're on the same team?"

On the way back to the office we swung by Renfroe's so I could pick up a pound of pralines for Rosario, and when we got in I stayed on the phones all afternoon, helping Em and Rosario with the inbound calls about Karen's kidnapping. In this way I regained Rosario's favor.

The Chief swung by in the afternoon to see how we were doing. He was troubled because there still hadn't been a ransom call. As the day wore on without one it was harder to remain hopeful that it had been a financially motivated crime. The other possibilities seemed horrible. He also told us the hospital was keeping Joe for one more night as a precaution, but expected to release him the next day.

As soon as the phones closed at five o'clock, Emily came into my office and plopped down in the guest chair. "Between calls telling me how Karen was abducted by aliens and complaints about how we're overwatering Shoreline Park, I managed to do some research. Turns out there's only one mitigation bank in the tri-county area. It's here in Santa Rosa, up north in the Blackwater section. Owned and operated by one McKinley Deaver, who used to be the city planner for Milton. He's partial owner of a larger mitigation bank over toward Tallahassee, also. That one's older. The new one is 200 acres up by Jay, just west of the Blackwater River State Forest. Mr. Deaver's website says he bought the acreage in Santa Rosa because he wanted to apply sound mitigation practices in his home county, where there's great economic pressure to develop coastal land."

"How noble. Let's go."

Jay was an hour north of Gulf Breeze. To get there we had to take the Garcon Point Bridge across Pensacola Bay, then stay on 87 until we were almost in Alabama.

It never ceased to amaze me how different north Santa Rosa County was from the southern part of the county, and how different both were from neighboring Escambia County to the west.

Gulf Breeze and the rest of south Santa Rosa were of course part of the Redneck Riviera, supporting Pensacola Beach's modest tourist trade. Rich or poor, many of the residents were there for the Salt Life—the proximity to the gulf and other coastal waters, and all the opportunities for fishing, boating, jetskiing, sunbathing, and daydreaming they afforded. Many south Santa Rosa residents were former military. They'd been stationed on the panhandle at some point during their service, at one of the bases—the Naval Air Station in Pensacola, Whiting Field in Milton, Eglin Air Force Base in Fort Walton, or Tyndall Air Force Base near Panama City—and fallen in love with the beautiful beaches, the amazing water views that surround us everywhere, and the affordable cost of living. Fallen in love and vowed to come back. Which they did, in quiet droves, after retiring from active duty.

My father, Keith, was one of them. Originally from Mississippi, he'd joined the Army in '78. The country was still stinging from the aftermath of Vietnam, and military service wasn't a popular choice in other areas of the country, but the Deep South continued to supply cannon fodder in disproportionate numbers. At the age of 19, wanting to get out of town, Keith had signed up for a two-year stint.

It only took a few days for Keith Maddox to realize the military wasn't for him, but he stuck it out, and when his unit was sent to the Naval Air Station for training, he felt his otherwise pointless service had served a purpose after all: it exposed him to the Salt Life. He fell in love with the panhandle immediately. Eighteen months later, when his discharge was complete, he found a shack to rent on the edge of a swamp bordering the Live Oaks, leased a lift in a local garage, and hung out his sign as a mechanic. After that he tinkered expertly with engines. Any engines: in cars, boats, motorcycles, or RVs, it didn't matter to Keith, he'd work on them just as he had in the military and as a boy back home in Meridian, Mississippi, before that. He put in just enough hours to pay his meager bills and spent the rest of his time fishing, shelling, sunbathing, and partying out at the beach.

He was popular with the ladies on the Pensacola Beach dating scene. He was tall, fit, blond, and blue-eyed, so no wonder. But he always told me his playboy days were over the day he met Lindsey Carmen.

Keith was 24 when they met, Lindsey 17. In the photos from back then, Lindsey has curtains of brown, flat-ironed hair and delicate features. When they met she was hanging out with a group of older girls, several of whom were already on intimate terms with Keith.

He said she barely spoke when they were in a group together, but everything she did say was very funny—often in an aside just for him. And when she laughed, it was a loud, unembarrassed giggle, completely different from the other girls' suppressed chuckles, which they thought signaled their sophistication.

Keith was so smitten that when Lindsey told him, after they'd been semi-shacking up together for a few weeks, that she was pregnant, he was delighted. In direct violation of his lease, he painted each of the rooms in his little rental house a different pastel color, then hung a solar system mural in the yellow room he intended to be the nursery.

But as it turned out, Lindsey wasn't as taken with domesticity as Keith. She did stick around to breastfeed me for six months. After that, she took off for California in a VW Vanagon with a bunch of surfers.

I saw her a grand total of three more times after that, until I was 15, when we got word that she'd been found dead in a motel room in Redwood City, California.

Keith never said, but I'd figured out the problem a couple years before that on my own. It was simple, really. Lindsey just had a stronger taste for cocaine than she did for family life.

It's okay, though. Keith was worth a dozen mothers, as far as I was concerned.

In contrast to the Salt Life of south Santa Rosa, the country where we were headed now was pure cracker south. Loblolly pine and scrub oak forests, peanut and soybean farms, trailers, rusty cars permanently raised on blocks, Confederate flags in picture windows. There'd been a brief boom in the '80s, when a field up by Jay started producing oil and natural gas and made millionaires of a few of the soybean farmers. But eventually the field ran dry, the neighbors stopped prospecting, and everyone went back to farming.

We'd picked up Whataburger again on our way out of town. For the first part of the drive we silently ate our burgers and fries and listened to the radio. After we'd driven north on 89 for about 15 miles, I turned the radio down.

"What now? Do I head into Jay?"

Jay was the only incorporated city in north Santa Rosa. It had a population of 700 and one streetlight. If you sneezed you would miss it.

"No. Actually, take this right up here. We need to head toward Munson."

I made the turn and in doing so left behind the civilized conveniences of painted lane lines and mile markers. We rode through peanut fields in the deepening shadows of the fast-approaching dusk.

"Is this even a public road?" I asked Emily.

"Dunno. Just drive it with confidence."

A few miles later we hit a T. After consulting her map and a nest of papers, Emily suggested I make a left. I did so. Now we were headed northwest on another country road, with peanut fields on our left and pine forest on our right. A couple more miles and Emily said, "I think we should be there."

"How will we know? It's not like they're going to have a 'Welcome to the Mitigation Bank' sign up, right?"

"I don't know. Slow down a little."

I did so. Emily rolled down her window and stared out. Then, "There!" she said.

I looked where she was pointing. Sure enough, a small sign was planted by the roadside, next to a dirt road turnoff.

Property of Mitigation Solutions, LLC
Dedicated to restoring and maintaining adequate
wetlands on the Florida Panhandle.

There was a phone number on the sign. Em wrote down the number and the business name while I turned onto the dirt road.

The road alternated between potholes and washboard bumps. We were walled in by pine and scrub oak on both sides. After half a mile we reached a clearing. It was about the size of a football field and more or less circular. I pulled a quarter of the way around the circle and parked.

There was still light out but it was fading fast. We both climbed out of the truck. Emily immediately set off around the perimeter of the circle, headed counter-clockwise. She touched the trunks of trees, bent and peered at ground plants, tore leaves off, and sniffed. She was like the Plant Whisperer. I had no idea what she was doing, but I set off in the other direction, hoping to make myself useful or at least to stay out of Emily's way until she was ready to communicate.

I crossed the opening to the dirt road we'd come in on and was continuing around the circle when something on the ground caught my eye. A flash of white, like a discarded piece of paper. Not unusual back in civilization, but unlikely here. I bent and picked it up.

It *was* a piece of paper. A fragment, actually, covered with text. When I started skimming it seemed familiar, until I realized it was a printout of the page from the Panhandlers for Change website Em had shown me earlier that day.

"Em! Look at this!" I ran across the clearing to Emily, who was making notes on her little legal pad and wearing a frowny face.

"I have news for you," Em said. "There's no mitigating going on here. This landscape is the same ecosystem as the upland portions of the Blackwater River State Forest. Very nice greenspace. But not wetlands."

"Oh. Well, I have this," I said, showing her my little piece of paper.

Neither Em nor I was able to get a cell signal out in the Mitigation Solutions field, but once we were back on the road and had driven a few miles south, my phone picked up my network. I called The Chief and told him what we'd found. He said he'd be in touch with the sheriffs in Milton and Jay about focusing search efforts for Karen up in north Santa Rosa. He also asked me for directions, saying he intended to head up to the field immediately himself. I handed the phone to Em. She read off the driving directions to him. There was a pause and then she laughed and said, "They can wait!" Then she hung up.

"What was that all about?" I asked.

"The Chief says we shouldn't keep our husbands waiting too long."

★ ★ ★ ★ ★

I dropped Em off in the office parking lot so she could pick up her car. We waved our goodbyes and I headed home, where Chris had dinner ready and was still using the same cell phone. All was well on the home front. But as I got ready for bed, I found myself thinking of Karen, a woman I'd never met but now felt an intense sympathy for. For the second night in a row she wouldn't be sleeping at home in her own bed. Where was she? What was she doing? Would she be all right?

CHAPTER TEN

When Karen awoke, daylight was just beginning to filter into the musty house. The light still had that gray, gritty quality that meant the sun wasn't fully up yet. Just after dawn, then.

She took stock. Her head ached, but not in the excruciating way it had the day before. This pain was manageable. A person could work on an escape plan through a headache like this one.

She was on the red couch with an afghan tossed over her. Her hands and feet were tied, but her captor had allowed her to lie on her back this time, meaning her arms were tied in front of her. Yesterday, before she'd passed out, she'd vowed to herself that she would wake up before him and start working on the hand restraints, which she thought she could get loose with a little time. Now, though, as she opened her eyes and looked around the room, she saw she was too late—he was already sitting in the chair, eyes glinting in the dim light, gun on his knees.

Damn, Karen thought, angry with herself for not trying harder to escape the day before. Then she remembered her promise to herself. *Let it go.*

"You want some coffee?" the man asked.

"Yes."

He took a thermos from the end table beside him and filled a mug, which he placed on the trunk in front of her. Karen batted the afghan down with her tied hands and struggled to sit up.

"Here." He came over and untied her arms. Karen tried not

to shudder as he touched her. Again he stepped away as soon as her arms were loose. She rubbed her chafed wrists for a moment, then picked up the coffee mug and sipped. Not bad. She drank some more and felt her headache start to recede.

Her captor sipped his coffee, too, then rose with a sigh and walked out of the room, limping slightly.

Karen set her mug down, pushed the afghan aside, and looked down at the ropes on her legs. They were expertly tied. Her circulation remained decent, but there wasn't a lot of give between the ropes and her skin—maybe a matchstick's worth. But having her hands untied meant it was a whole different story. She didn't intend to squander any more escape opportunities as she had yesterday.

She didn't want to panic either, though. She studied the ropes for a moment, learning the patterns they formed as they snaked around her legs. When she thought she had a good place to start working, she reached down.

"I wouldn't do that," a voice said. She looked up. Her kidnapper was across the room, holding the gun up, pointing it at her. He began to cross toward her, keeping the gun up at face level.

"I don't want to kill you; you're no use to me dead. But I will if I have to."

Karen weighed her options. He was still limping and looked frail. Should she rush him? He was probably an ace shot, though. He was clearly a country man, someone who undoubtedly knew how to clean a fish and tie a proper knot—and shoot a gun.

The question was, would he hesitate at all if she came after him? That could mean the difference between whether she lived or died. She looked in his eyes.

It's always hard to tell, of course, what really lives in the hearts of others. But her best guess was: hell yes he would. Shoot her, that is. If it came down to it he would probably kill her without question. There was something not right about his expression. And it seemed like they were way out in the woods somewhere; he probably wouldn't have much trouble making her body disappear.

If she thought he intended to rape or torture her, she would try harder to escape. But despite the fact that he seemed off somehow, his proclivities didn't seem to lie in that direction. Though the phrase "no use to me" still made her shudder.

He seemed to sense what she was thinking. "I won't make use of you like that," he said, grimacing. "If that's what I was after, I would have picked someone younger. Anyway, that's a sinful thing. What we're going to do is righteous."

Oh great. Crazy religious, sexually mixed up—this didn't sound good, though she almost exploded with laughter at the "someone younger" comment.

Crazy guy seemed to have gotten himself all flustered with this speech. "I'll show you. Come on."

Karen looked at him. He'd flustered himself so badly he seemed to have forgotten that her legs were tied. What was she supposed to do, hop?

"Oh, right." He came over and crouched beside her to untie her legs. Karen kept her head turned away and breathed through her mouth, trying not to gag. Judging from the smell of it, he didn't bathe too often. But more than that, she was just completely, skin-crawlingly skeeved out whenever he came near her.

However, once again he merely untied the ropes then stepped away. Karen reached down and rubbed her sore legs, waiting for circulation to return. When she stood up she was wobbly for a moment, but then she steadied herself.

Looking back down at her feet, she noticed her Tevas lined up neatly under the couch. Both of them. She felt her heart sink. She'd been hoping the lost sandal might serve as a clue for anyone looking for her. But he must have noticed it missing while she was unconscious and gone back out to retrieve it, just as he'd taken the turtle shell from her when they were on the beach—with a jolt she remembered that detail, forgotten until now. He must have conked her on the head immediately afterward.

Discouraged by his thoroughness, she tried to compose herself. The man watched in silence until she looked up at him, indicating she was ready.

"This way," he said. He led her down a narrow hallway toward the back of the house, where the bedrooms and bathrooms were. Despite his reassurance, and the fact that he'd touched her as briefly as possible while untying her, Karen felt a twinge. Was this going to turn out to be sexual after all? Had she miscalculated?

The man stopped in a doorway and stepped aside, indicating Karen should enter the room. When she peeked in there were no signs of instruments of torture or restraint. There wasn't even a bed. Instead, a large oak desk was placed in the middle of the room, with a comfy-looking office chair behind it. An old manual Underwood typewriter was centered on the table, in front of the chair. There was a ream of paper, a bottle of whiteout, and a stack of newspapers.

Karen looked at the man in confusion.

"Time to get to work," he said.

CHAPTER ELEVEN

When I got to the office the next morning, Rosario was at her workstation and Emily was at the counter, deep in conversation with a couple of residents. They were a stocky, middle-aged man with thinning hair and hands thrust into his jean pockets, and a tiny woman with tufty hair who somewhat resembled Snoopy's friend Woodstock from the old Peanuts comics. Probably the guy's mother, I decided, after comparing their faces.

Rosario made eyes at me as I crossed the front office, indicating she thought it might be a good idea for me to get involved in the discussion. It didn't seem heated, but I recognized Emily's patient voice. I nodded at Rosario to indicate I understood and continued back to my office, where I shed my jacket and purse and left my lunch box on the desk.

I grabbed a fence permit application and returned to the outer office, where I positioned myself at the service counter and pretended to review the application. This way I could get up to speed on the situation without drawing attention to myself.

"It's not that you *can't* subdivide your lot," Emily was saying to the mother and son. "But you can't do so using the application Mr. Perry submitted because his application was for all these lots." She pointed down to the plat in her hand, which showed a proposed 12-lot subdivision tentatively named Breezy Meadows.

Ah, so that was it. Guy Perry was a well-established panhandle developer. He'd started applications for three separate small

93

residential subdivisions in Gulf Breeze during the past year, which perplexed me. New projects had become very scarce; it was unheard of for a developer to start work on three new projects at once in our post-bubble economy.

Guy had taken all three of the projects as far as preliminary approval from the Planning Commission, which he duly received—and then they'd died on the vine. When I expressed surprise, Mike said Guy was just keeping his options open in case the economy started showing signs of a turnaround. After all, getting a project to the preliminary approval stage only involved an investment of a few thousand dollars—pocket change to someone like Guy, especially since he was a licensed engineer who could work up the preliminary plats himself.

The problem was, he'd gotten some property owners involved with the new projects. This was common with infill development, which was practically all that was left in Gulf Breeze, given our small land mass. There were still undeveloped parcels of land, but not many large enough to create a whole new subdivision from scratch. Therefore most of our new residential development came in the form of infill, where developers would design a project that combined undeveloped land with developed parcels to create a new subdivision. In doing so, they would of course have to get the existing property owners to agree—which they did in the usual way, with money. Often property lines would have to be redrawn so the developer could get maximum density while allowing existing residents to keep their houses and meet setback requirements. The developer would pay those residents for anything that was shaved off their lot size, and then throw a little more on top, just for good measure.

This kind of infill design was one of Guy Perry's specialties. But when he worked up three of them at once, and didn't follow up on any, it was inevitable that he'd left some residents disappointed. Given the fact that Breezy Meadows was little more than a concept, when Perry spoke to the property owners whose lots he hoped to use in it, in the interests of complete honesty he would have needed to couch things in very hypothetical terms: we might, they might, you might. As in: we might make a subdivision, they might approve it, you might make some money as a result. He would need to stress that the approval process was a long one, and that both the Planning Commission and the City Council would have to review and approve the application before the subdivision became official.

And yet, if he was at all good at his job—and Perry *was* good—at the same time he would have spun a delicate web of hope in the minds of the residents as he talked to them about the advantages of participating in his project. It would have been a web spun out of money. The problem was, once a developer started talking to certain residents about money . . . well. There are, of course, citizens everywhere for whom there's no real distinction between money in their imagination and money in the bank. The residents to whom Emily was now speaking evidently fell into this category. Somehow they'd gone from enjoying a fantasy about the hypothetical money they might make from their portion of Breezy Meadows to counting on that money. Who knows, they might even have *spent* the money, in the form of buying on credit, or otherwise increasing their debt.

But now Guy Perry was in the wind, no longer taking their phone calls. Breezy Meadows was just an idea he'd had, one of many, and the fact that he'd let the project go dormant meant he'd determined there was no money to be made from it, at least for now. He might pick it up again in five years, or ten, if the real estate market turned again. Or he might never give Breezy Meadows another thought in his life.

In the meantime, the two residents who were in the office had probably thought of little else since Guy had showed up on their doorstep spinning fairy tales. So they'd come down to the office to see if they could make some of that wonderful, magical money Mr. Perry had conjured, even without his help.

Hypothetically, it might be possible for them to subdivide their lot, all by itself, thus creating a little two-lot subdivision. That's evidently what Emily was looking into, as she turned to the plat drawers and pulled out a plat. She unfolded it and stood examining it for a few minutes, nodded her head, then turned back toward the counter. She set the plat on the counter, pointed to a section, leaned over toward the residents, and began speaking.

I moved a little closer. The plat Em had pulled was for Pine Circle, an old subdivision from the '70s. That portion of the city hadn't even been annexed yet when Pine Circle was developed, meaning the subdivision had been created under county guidelines and was therefore pretty much up for grabs, in terms of city development. Perry had planned to use half the lots from Pine Circle, plus some adjoining undeveloped land, for his Breezy Meadows creation.

"You said you live at 324 Shirley?" Emily asked the residents. They nodded. "Okay, here's your lot." She pointed down at the plat. "This area is zoned R-1-20, meaning lots in a subdivision with this zoning must maintain an average of 20,000 square feet, with no lot smaller than 16,000 square feet. Also, each lot must have at least 110 feet of frontage.

"It looks like you're on an acre and it's a corner lot, so it shouldn't be hard to meet the square footage and frontage requirements. The house is placed over to one side, which is good. You would need to have an engineer work up a plat showing the proposed lot line. If you want to keep your existing house, the engineer will have to show that it can meet the setback requirements."

"Mr. Perry said there would be no trouble for us to keep our house."

"Well, yes," Em said, placing the proposed Breezy Meadows plat in front of the residents. "But remember, he had more land to work with. As you can see here, he was using the adjacent land to redraw your lot line, to make sure your house stayed within code. See, he's got your house drawn on here. And see how your north side lot line was going to move, compared to where it is on the recorded plat? But if you're creating a two-lot subdivision from your lot alone, then that's a whole new project, and what Mr. Perry proposed with Breezy Meadows doesn't apply. Unless you persuaded some of your neighbors to work on the project with you. But either way—whether it involves just your lot or several others—you would need to start the application process over. This packet walks you through the process."

Em held out a rather thick sheaf of papers to the residents. They seemed disinclined to take it. They looked at her with suspicion and dislike, as though she were trying to cheat them out of their profits. I thought she'd explained things fairly well. But that's how it was, once a developer had gotten into a resident's head.

Finally, the old lady reached over and took the packet from Emily, more out of pity than anything else. If they bothered to look at it closely, they would see that they were likely to be out around $12,000 before they saw even a glimmer of hope for selling the second lot they wanted to create. And that would be the end of that.

"So you're saying we *can* subdivide our lot and sell the second lot?" the man asked.

"Yes. I mean, it looks like it, though you'll want an engineer to work up some drawings, showing that the square footage, frontage, and setback requirements can all be met. But judging from what the Pine Circle plat shows, it looks like you have enough square footage and frontage to move forward. This packet tells what you need to do at each step. First, you'll want to schedule an appointment to come to our weekly Development Review meeting." Em picked up another copy of the Subdivision packet she had nearby and flipped to the second page. "This page shows what you'll bring to the DR meeting and the fees. You can call me when you're ready, and we'll get that scheduled."

"Fees?"

"Yes. There are fees associated with each stage of the application. After the DR meeting you'll need to go before the Planning Commission. If the Planning Commission recommends the project, you'll go to City Council for final approval."

"And then we can sell the second lot?"

"As soon as the public improvements are complete, yes."

"What do you mean, public improvements?"

"Gulf Breeze requires that each lot in a new subdivision have a sewer connection, as well as curb/gutter/sidewalk. But that's probably already in place."

"Not on Plantation," I piped up, referring to the side street where the residents wanted to create the frontage for their second lot.

"Oh," Em said, throwing me a despairing glance before turning back to the residents. "Then you'll need to complete curb/gutter/sidewalk along this side."

"Mr. Perry didn't say nothing about that," the male resident said with disgust. "C'mon, Mom."

They shuffled out of the office. Em looked crestfallen.

"Don't worry. You did great."

"I just feel bad they're so disappointed. I don't think they can afford to subdivide."

"You told them what they needed to know," Rosario said suddenly. "It's not your fault Guy Perry filled their head with unrealistic expectations. They need to know what they're getting into. I've seen homeowners try to subdivide and it's usually a mess. They get in way over their heads. They wind up in debt— I've seen couples divorce over it. Better that they know now."

Rosario smiled at Emily. I assumed this spirited defense meant Rosario was no longer mad at us for our long absences from the office lately. Which was a good thing because I planned on spiriting Emily away again during our lunch break today.

"I don't mean *they're* a married couple," Rosario added, looking out the window, where the disgruntled residents had just emerged from the building and were crossing the parking lot. "That's Paula Harris and her son, Ryan. He's just pushing her to subdivide because he wants the money. Not that they'd make any money in this economy, anyway. I don't know what Paula's thinking, letting him push her around like that." Rosario shook her head and turned back to her filing.

I signed off on the fence permit application I'd been using as a prop and handed it to Emily. "This one's good to go—you can call Ms. McDaniel and tell her she can pick it up." Then I mouthed, "Lunch." Em nodded.

I went back to my office and put in a few hours of steady work. I reviewed more fence permit applications, did some filing, wrote a few code violation letters, and then wrote letters to the residents who'd filed the code complaints in the first place, letting them know what steps I was taking to rectify the situations they'd reported. Some residents who reported code violations preferred to do so anonymously; others expected almost hourly reports on one's progress.

At 11 o'clock, I heard Rosario tell Emily she was leaving for lunch. A moment later, Emily's head appeared in my door.

"What's up?"

"I think we need to go see Mr. Deaver."

"The owner of Mitigation Solutions? Love the idea, but can

we get all the way there and back in an hour?"

"His office isn't in Milton. It's in Portofino. Tower Three."

While Rosario was at lunch I sat at her workstation and answered her phone. It was my attempt to mitigate our planned absence by making sure she didn't have a stack of callbacks waiting for her when she got back.

As soon as she returned and was settled at her workstation, Em and I headed out. I did a quick pass through the Whataburger drive-thru, then aimed for the beach. At Portofino Tower Three I pulled into the lot and parked.

"I didn't realize there were offices here," Emily said.

"Me neither. But no one ever wants to live on the ground floor of these places, so it's a good use of the space."

"Mixed use," Em said.

"Showoff," I teased. Em liked trotting out the planning and zoning vocabulary she was learning from Mike and me.

In the lobby we found a business directory engraved on a brass plate. Mitigation Solutions was in Suite 103. We followed an arrow down a short hall. The main lobby was fancy but Suite 103 just had a plain wooden door.

Emily stopped. "Do you think they're even here?"

I grabbed the knob and turned. The door opened. "Yup."

Inside there was a small reception area featuring green wallpaper patterned with large pink roses and black carpet adorned with a smaller floral pattern. In the midst of this kinetic background sat a wood veneer desk with a large basket of artificial flowers on it. There was a black office chair behind the desk and one purplish upholstered waiting room chair against the opposite wall.

We stood and stared for a moment. "This is the least inviting waiting room I've ever seen in my life," Em said finally. "It's like a blind person decorated it."

"Or a man," I muttered.

"Hello?" A male voice spoke from an inner room.

"Hi! We're looking for Mr. Deaver?"

"You found him," the voice said, emerging from the hallway. Deaver was a huge man, probably 6′ 5″ and at least 300 pounds. I guessed he was late 40s, with thinning blond hair and bright blue eyes. He was wearing a blue suit, a checkered shirt with a bolo tie, and work boots. The country gentleman. The farmer-professional.

Deaver quickly took us in. "What can I do for you lovely ladies?"

I did the introductions, then explained, "We were hoping to ask you a couple of questions about Mitigation Solutions."

"That's funny, the police were just here asking me the same thing," Deaver said. "That's why you caught me here in the of-fice—normally I'm not here much. Come on back. I always have time for a couple of pretty women."

He led us down a short hall to his office. It was larger than the reception area, with a window looking to the west. There was a stretch of empty beach out there and condos visible in the distance, as well as a little slice of the gulf water. Not the best view Portofino offered. But probably not the worst, either.

The office housed an L-shaped desk of far superior quality to the one in the reception area. Laptop, combination printer/copier/scanner, and several messy piles of paper were scattered around on the desk. On the wall there was an inspirational poster featuring a picture of a Boston terrier and a Great Dane, as well as a framed golf score card. Also, Mr. Deaver's diploma from FSU, showing he'd earned a master's degree in regional and urban planning.

The office included two comfortable-looking guest chairs. Deaver gestured for us to sit.

"FSU," I said. "Right on. I did a planning B.A. there."

"Go Noles," Deaver said. "It's so weird that you gals stopped by. I just got finished talking to your chief of police—Tad To-bin? He and I go way back. My brother Dave played high school football against him, back in the day. Anyway, evidently a woman was kidnapped from the beach just east of here on Wednesday, and Tad thinks the kidnapper has some interest in my company. Some evidence was found on my property north of Milton, that the guy might have been there before he snatched this poor woman. Crazy, huh?"

Deaver smiled. He was concentrating on me, treating me like the Alpha.

You had to give these Good Old Boys credit. While being perfectly affable, he was letting us know he was already completely familiar with the situation and had guessed why we were there. Had The Chief told him it was two women from the office who'd found evidence of the kidnapper on Deaver's property? It was definitely possible, in which case he no doubt realized we were the two women.

There was a subtext to his message too, of course. Stay out of it, y'all. The Boys have this one under control.

But I knew how to play the Good Old Boy game, too. I briefly returned his smile, then just as quickly wiped the smile from my face, replacing it with a tragic look. "Isn't it terrible? The Chief's been telling us a little about what's going on with the kidnapping investigation. In fact, Emily knows Karen Baretta, the woman who was kidnapped." I gestured toward Em, who nodded, though her brow was all knotted up. She didn't like these reindeer games.

"I'm sorry about your friend," Deaver said.

"Yes, it's very worrisome," Emily said. "I'm worried about Joe, too—Karen's husband. He was hurt during the kidnapping Wednesday. And now he's just beside himself. He's very devoted to Karen."

"That's what I hear."

"It *is* terrible about Karen," I said, wanted to get us back on track. "We're all praying that she's found quickly and comes home safe. But I'm embarrassed to admit—as a planner—that this incident is the first I'd heard of mitigation banks. I mean, I think I have a vague memory they might have been mentioned in one of Dr. Thresher's wetlands classes. But I had no idea we had any mitigation banks in Santa Rosa."

"It's very new," Deaver said. "I just went through the process of creating the bank last year. Made an offer on the land, got special zoning approval from the County. I also had to file applications with the state and the Army Corps of Engineers."

"But it's uplands," Em blurted. "How can it possibly be used to offset wetlands development?"

"Well, now, Little Lady, that's because we haven't mitigated it yet. We're just getting started. The Blackwater River site will be used to ensure Santa Rosa County doesn't lose another single net acre of wetlands, moving forward."

"But isn't future wetlands development likely to occur in South Santa Rosa, down by the Gulf and the Sound?" Emily persisted. "How will mitigation 50 miles north help water filtration and drainage down by the beach—assuming you can even turn that land up there into a floodplain?"

"Somebody's done their homework," Deaver said. There was a note of irritation in his voice, though he smiled. "I assure you the ecosystem north of Redfish Cove affects that to the south. Remember, everything in this area drains south to the Gulf. And pollution in the groundwater is a much bigger problem in northern Escambia and Santa Rosa Counties, as I'm sure Ms. LaRue here can tell you. So actually, introducing a filtration plain in north Santa Rosa is beneficial to the whole community. You know, if you like clean water."

Em seemed likely to continue the fight, but I thought this inadvisable. I sprang to my feet. "Thank you for your time," I said, sticking out my hand. "This has been so helpful. I really learned a lot."

I hustled Em out to the lobby. Once there, however, I smacked myself on the forehead. "My purse! Be right back."

Em gave me a startled look but before she could say anything I was back at Deaver's office door, which was now closed. I rapped a couple of times, then opened it quickly. As I expected, he was on the phone.

"Well this isn't Australia!" he shouted, before his eyes fell on me. I saw his character clearly in that moment. He more or less wanted to kill me.

Pretending not to notice, I pointed at the chair where I'd been sitting, which still held my green leather purse. "Sorry," I mouthed, shrugging my shoulders and rolling my eyes, doing my Blondie act, before grabbing the purse and skedaddling.

Emily was quiet until we were back in the truck. "What was that all about?"

"I wanted to see what he'd do after we left."

"And?"

"He was on the phone. Telling someone this isn't Australia."

"What does that mean?"

"I don't know. I was hoping you did."

"No idea," Emily said, frowning. "But this is the second time Australia has come up this week. It was on the watershed blog, too."

"I know."

"That can't be a coincidence."

"Nope."

Em tugged on her lip for a minute. "Did you mean it when you told Deaver you'd learned a lot?"

"Sure. I learned which agencies have to approve a mitigation bank around here. I learned how having the mitigation bank 50 miles away from the area where development is occurring is justified. I learned mitigation banks are run by the Good Old Boy network, at least in Santa Rosa County."

"No surprise there."

"No. But now we know for sure."

"I'd like to know what the going rate is for an acre of mitigated land. As well as what he paid for that land in the first place."

"You want to know the profit margin?"

Emily nodded.

"What I'd like is to go see that other mitigation bank Deaver is part owner of, over toward Tallahassee. See if there's any actual mitigating going on over there. You know what that means, little lady?"

"Road trip!"

CHAPTER TWELVE

Karen sat at her little desk, sipping tea and staring at the piece of paper placed in front of her. She still couldn't quite believe her predicament.

She'd been kidnapped in order to write letters to the editor.

It turned out her captor, whom she was now calling, by mutual agreement, "Bud," had a bee in his bonnet about wetlands preservation and mitigation banks. Well, that was fine; in fact, Karen thought it admirable. She had the same bee in her bonnet herself. The problem was, Bud was also a disenfranchised redneck with conspiracy theorist tendencies. As a result, over time he'd persuaded himself that he needed his own personal spokesperson to deliver his message to the world. And as the most visible environmental activist in their area, Karen was naturally his first choice.

At least, this was Bud's reasoning and the sequence of events, so far as Karen had been able to piece them together.

When she'd suggested that perhaps he could have simply approached her and asked for help writing the letters, instead of resorting to a Class A felony, Bud had muttered that people like her never took people like him seriously.

Ever since they'd held this conversation the day before, Karen had been trying to decide whether it was true. On the one hand, she and Bud seemed to be in perfect accord regarding their ideas about mitigation banks. They both thought they were bunk. Dangerous, criminal bunk.

And yet, she had to admit he had a point. If he'd approached her about collaborating on an education campaign about the folly of trying to mitigate wetlands, she probably would have turned him down.

Not for any of the reasons he thought, though. Not because he hadn't gone to college or because he chewed tobacco and spoke with a drawl and was, basically, a redneck. She had worked alongside plenty of self-proclaimed Florida crackers on environmental issues in her time. Some of them had been great comrades.

No, the reason she would have put him off was because there was a creepy vibe about him. Something a little too obsessed, too desperate. Even Karen, who thought about environmental issues pretty much all the time, thought so. He set off her internal sociopath radar.

Or did she only think so now because he had, in fact, kidnapped her, thus definitively establishing his sociopath status? It was hard to say for sure, but Karen didn't think so. He had an aura about him. The kind of thing that's hard to define, but that leads healthier sorts to stay away from the Buds of the world. Vincent Van Gogh might have had such an aura. And Mark David Chapman.

Karen shook her head and looked back down at her letter. She was being treated decently, at least. Given decent things to eat and drink, privacy in the bathroom, and plenty of time to work on her anti-mitigation bank message.

Writing the letter wasn't a problem, of course. She could pull arguments and statistics about mitigation banks out of her ass all day long. However, a couple of times yesterday she'd told Bud she had an idea but needed some research done. She was hoping to get him out of the house, but instead he'd retired to one of the back rooms, leading Karen to conclude that, unlikely though it seemed, there was Internet access in this crackerbox.

Actually she supposed it made sense. What modern age conspiracy theorist could live without high-speed Internet access in the home? Even if it meant he had to pay a satellite company an arm and a leg to get it.

By giving Bud these little assignments she was also testing his Internet and research savvy. She asked questions for which she knew he could come up with an answer, but only after a little digging. He was able to produce results in an impressively short time. She supposed that made sense, too. You couldn't be a modern-day conspiracy theorist without honing your Internet search skills.

When he disappeared to do research, or for other purposes, Bud would come into Karen's work room and tie up something—tie one of her hands to the desk, or bind her legs together—but this became more perfunctory each time. He'd told her they were far from the road, and that if she tried to escape, he would find her and shoot her before she reached it. She more or less believed him. She was keeping her eyes out for a method and time of escape—she didn't want to become complacent. But as long as she wasn't being threatened with sexual or physical harm, she was willing to wait it out a little.

Her main worry right now was Joe. He must be frantic, scared to death about her and blaming himself for her disappearance. That was part of the reason she was lingering so long over the first letter.

It was a shame, too, because Joe himself would have been so much better at this work than she was. Though she could churn out letters to the editor, petitions, and leaflets with the best of them, Joe was the one who loved crosswords and acrostics and other word puzzles.

But it had to be done. She sighed and looked down at the letter again, trying to figure out how to work the secret message

KAREN BARETTA into the text of her composition without alerting Bud.

Chapter Thirteen

I don't like to talk in the morning. If I had my way, I wouldn't even utter my first syllable of the day until I've been up for a couple of hours—except on days when something dreadful, like the necessity of having to go to work, intervenes.

Chris, on the other hand, seems to wake up in the middle of an ongoing conversation every morning. He just opens his eyes and starts talking. I couldn't believe it, when we first moved in together. No one in my family had ever been like that. When I was growing up, Keith and I would sometimes go a whole day without saying a word to each other. Not out of anger. Just because there was nothing we needed to say.

To maintain peace in our household, Chris and I have arrived at a compromise schedule when it comes to morning chatter. During the week, I tend to be a little stressed while I'm getting ready for work, so Chris lets me be. But on weekend mornings, Chris is allowed to talk to his heart's content—as long as he makes breakfast.

The terms of our agreement specify that I'm not obliged to respond, nor even really to listen, during these monologues, as long as I don't shut them down.

". . . So then Driscoll tells us there've been complaints from the staff that those of us teaching lower grades aren't sufficiently preparing the kids for eighth grade. I knew it had to be Morton. So I went and hunted him down as soon as we got out of the meeting. I said, 'Jim, what's the deal?' And he didn't even deny it. Instead he tries to kiss my ass. He said, 'I specifically told him I didn't mean you, Chris. You're a great teacher. It's the language arts staff. The kids get to my class and they can't read the textbook.' I guess he thought that was going to make me his buddy. But you don't do that, you don't suck up to a new administrator by throwing your fellow teachers under a bus. Now Driscoll's calling this special meeting, like we don't have enough meetings already . . ."

Chris set a plate of bacon and scrambled eggs in front of me where I sat in our breakfast nook, drinking coffee. Still talking, he poured out a glass of the concoction he'd just whipped up in the juicer, a strawberry banana smoothie with a yogurt and orange juice base, and set that in front of me as well. I picked up the glass and took a long gulp. It was delicious.

Chris came back to the table with a plate and a glass of his own and wolfed down his breakfast. As soon as he'd finished he jumped up and set his plate in the sink, came back over for a kiss, then departed for basketball practice in the community league where he coached. He never stopped talking the entire time.

After he left I finished my breakfast and had one more cup of coffee. Then I took a quick shower and threw a few things in an overnight bag. Only then, while I was washing up the dishes, did I utter my first words of the day. They were addressed to The Chief, who I called for a status update before heading out.

He didn't have much to report. The crime scene techs were up at the Mitigation Solutions site, poking around. They hadn't found much yet except tire tracks belonging to a late model, natural gas–powered F-150 and shoeprints of two women, one tall, one petite.

"Shoot. Sorry."

"Don't be. We might never have known to head up there if it wasn't for you and that little sidekick of yours. Anyway, one of the techs did find a separate tire track. Might belong to our kidnapper, might not. We know it doesn't belong to any of Deaver's vehicles, though."

"He doesn't drive a panel van?"

The Chief snorted. "Actually this tire's a real generic after-market brand. Probably on some kind of sedan, the tech said, but aside from that it didn't give us much. The Escambia County lab's running it through some databases, though, just for the fun of it. And they're checking it against some imprints they took down at the beach where Karen was grabbed."

I asked The Chief to keep me posted, then signed off and headed out to the truck. Though it wasn't nine o'clock yet, the sun was already hot on top of my head. I was wearing shorts, a t-shirt, and a hoodie, but when I got in the truck I rolled down the window and pulled the hoodie off. I grabbed a ponytail holder out of the truck's center console and flipped my hair up so it wouldn't whip into my face once we got on the highway. Then I backed out of the driveway and turned toward 98.

When I got to the 98 intersection, Polly spoke up. "Turn left," she said.

Polly was the GPS. Evidently Chris had come out to the truck last night and programmed in our itinerary. I still had to pick up Emily, though, so I made a right.

"You are going in the wrong direction," Polly said. I would have sworn there was a note of anxiety in her voice. "Make a U-turn as soon as possible."

"Oh hush," I said, turning the unit off.

Emily was standing on her porch when I pulled into her driveway. Her overnight bag rested on the porch swing, and she was leaning against the rail, smoking a cigarette and watching the birds at the feeder in her neighbors' yard.

When she saw me she hurriedly put the cigarette out, then picked up her bag and walked to the truck. She was wearing a sundress, a cardigan, and her prescription sunglasses. When she got in the car and saw my open window she took out an elastic and put her own hair up, then opened her window as well.

"You know what I wasn't doing?" she asked as I backed out of the driveway.

"Smoking?"

"That's right."

We were headed for Port St. Joe, three hours southeast of Gulf Breeze. The official purpose of the trip was a visit to Reclamation Acres, the other mitigation bank owned by McKinley Deaver. Reclamation Acres was on the western edge of the Apalachicola National Forest, and Port St. Joe was 30 miles south of it on the coast. We could have made it to the mitigation bank and back in one long day trip, but I'd suggested we pack bags and make it an overnighter, get a room at one of the little roadside motels in Port St. Joe. I'd been there for spring break once during college, and thinking about the area around Tallahassee had made me nostalgic to see the place again. Plus it had been a while since I'd had a night out with the girls.

I glanced over at Emily, who was peering intently down at the Florida road map in her lap. I didn't have the heart to tell her Polly knew exactly where we were going. It was mostly a straight shot east along the coast anyway. I wasn't sure why Chris had even bothered with the GPS. But then I decided to leave it off so as not to disappoint Emily. She's one of those people who loves maps.

Once we'd agreed to stay in Port St. Joe, I planned several more stops for our trip. Improbable though it might sound, some portions of the Redneck Riviera have become models of New Urbanism, the urban design movement that stresses mixed-use and walkable neighborhoods over automobile-centered, separate-use design. Several planned communities along the panhandle coast are prime examples of the movement. The most well known is Seaside, famous for being the town where the movie *The Truman Show* was filmed, but there's also Rosemary Beach and Sandestin. I'd taken field trips to these places as part of my coursework at FSU, but Emily had never seen them. Now that she was taking an interest in planning and zoning, I thought she should.

When we'd cleared the National Seashore, Emily looked up from her map. "I guess we just stay on 98 for a while."

"That's right, Polly."

"I'm hungry."

"I could go for a McMuffin myself," I said, despite Chris's bacon and eggs. We were coming up on a McDonald's. I turned the truck in.

Fifteen minutes later we were back on the road, the cab now full of the tantalizing smells of bacon grease and coffee. I punched on the radio and we quickly passed through the portion of Gulf Breeze to the east of the Naval Oaks.

Once we were out of Gulf Breeze, 98 opened up, and then for a while we were truly in the country. We rode through several miles of long leaf pine forest, interrupted only by the occasional house and a pawn shop with the word GUNS displayed prominently in the window. As we neared Navarre the subdivisions started again and 98 wound close to the Santa Rosa Sound, so we drove right along the water for a while. Then there was Hurlburt Field, the southernmost section of Eglin Air Force Base, a sprawling military compound covering more than 700 square miles.

"Where's the 19 acres Panhandlers for Change was protesting about?" I asked. "The ones Eglin wants to sell off without giving the National Seashore first dibs?"

"I dunno," Em said, looking startled. "I never really thought about it."

"It would be cool if we could go take a look."

"Definitely. I don't know how to find out, though. I'm afraid it would upset Joe if I called him to ask right now."

"True. Maybe another time."

After Hurlburt we crossed through tiny Mary Esther, where 98 was lined with live oaks, giving the town a graceful, antebellum feel. Then 98 skirted along the southern edge of Fort Walton Beach before sweeping over a bridge and out onto the next barrier island. Here there was another segment of the Gulf Islands National Seashore, so for a while it was all white, windswept dunes, scrub oak, and glimpses of the glimmering water. Then we crossed another bridge and entered Destin.

Destin is more upscale—and somewhat less rednecky—than Pensacola Beach. It still has a Costmart, though. Past the Costmart I pulled off 98 into a parking lot.

"What's this?" Em asked.

I pointed out the window at the sign: Donut Hole Café and Bakery.

"Can't drive past the Donut Hole without stopping."

A few minutes later we were back in the pickup. I had two glazed and Emily had a couple of chocolate rings.

"Third breakfast of the day," I said ruefully. "I'm going to have to dance an extra hour tonight."

East of Destin we passed through more rolling miles of longleaf pine forest until we reached the turnoff for 30A, which brought us to Seaside.

The town square was on our left. A walkway down to the beach was on our right. The narrow area between the road and the beach was densely filled with souvenir shops and restaurants. Though it was early in the season, the sidewalks were already thronging with tourists. Traffic on 30A was slowed to a crawl.

There was a horseshoe-shaped parking area surrounding the square. I spotted a lone open space and darted in.

"Huh," Emily said, once we were out of the truck. She stood

on the sidewalk, spinning slowly around, taking in the wood frame buildings, which looked properly picturesque under the clear blue sky. "It's smaller than I thought. I mean, it feels more cluttered."

"All the traffic doesn't help."

"Well, they should have planned for that, shouldn't they?"

We started walking up toward the top of the horseshoe. Em's enthusiasm increased when she saw Sundog Books housed on the main floor of one of the cute cottages. I played with the store dog, an ancient black Lab, while Emily browsed the shelves. She carried a couple of books around with her for a while but set them back down before rejoining me near the door.

"Aren't you going to get those?"

"Nah. I'll see if the library has them back home."

We continued around the horseshoe, passing a bar, a couple of restaurants, and a convenience store. At the base of the horseshoe, we came to a bulletin board for Seaside Community Realty. A poster showed the different styles of commercial cottages that were available and the prices. The smallest went for three hundred-fifty thousand; the largest, for well over a million.

"Damn," Emily said. "How many margaritas and margherita pizzas do you have to sell to pay off a million-dollar mortgage?"

The middle of the horseshoe was filled with a lush green lawn, like an old-fashioned village green. A white picket fence ran along the south side. At its exact center sat the Seaside Post Office, a tiny neoclassical structure combining the wood frame construction typical of the town with the architectural features of a Greek temple.

To either side of the Post Office, the picket fence was lined with evidence of how enterprising vendors had bypassed the million-dollar price tags set on local commercial property. Six Airstream trailers sparkled in the sun, three on each side of the

P.O. Lines of people were queued up in front of them; they appeared to be doing much brisker business than most of the shops housed in the expensive buildings.

"I would have liked to be a fly on the wall at the Planning Commission meeting where those trailers were approved," Emily said. "It must have been a bitter pill for the commissioners to swallow, realizing they needed to add trailers to their pristine downtown if they wanted commerce to flourish."

"I'm sure they mitigated it by specifying that the trailers had to be vintage Airstreams, polished to a blinding shine."

We strolled along the row of trailers. There was a barbeque place and a stand that sold Sno-cones. Then there was a stand advertising itself as a "Fruit Smoothie and Full Service Bar."

"Our Cukoo idea!" I said indignantly.

Cukoo Juice was a smoothie chain. It sold giant yogurt- or sherbet-based smoothies, to which you could add dietary supplements such as an "Energy Boost" or "Immunity Boost." There was a Cukoo near the UWF campus in Tallahassee, and when I was at school, a Banana Berry smoothie with an Energy Boost had been my favorite breakfast.

But there was no Cukoo Juice in Gulf Breeze or Pensacola, much to my sorrow. Whenever I had a bad day at work, I'd announce I was quitting Community Development and opening a Cukoo Juice out on Pensacola Beach instead. Emily always chimed in. "And I'll set up a stand right outside your Cukoo Juice, selling shots of rum and vodka for people to pour into their smoothies. And we'll see which one of us rakes in more money."

Now here in Seaside someone had combined our two ideas into one Airstream trailer of vacation refreshment perfection. We joined the line and a few minutes later were sipping rum-soaked smoothies. Then Emily exclaimed, "Cupcakes!" We stopped and gazed at "Queen Bee Cupcakes" in awe. "Another brilliant use of the Airstream trailer," Emily finally said. "I'm beginning to see the appeal of Seaside after all."

We joined the cupcake line. Moments later, Em was the happy owner of a Creamy Coconut, while I had a Vanilla Pink. We sat on the stairs of the Seaside Post Office, which was closed for renovations, and ate our cupcakes.

"That's the sweetest thing I've ever eaten in my life," Em said when she was finished. "My teeth are coming loose in my head. I feel sick."

"Sick, but happy."

We carried our drinks across the busy street to the beach side, where we browsed a couple of storefronts before crossing the walkway over the dunes. A flock of blue umbrellas shaded tourists from the sun. Aside from that, the water was green, the sand was white, the sky was blue, and the sun was dazzling, just like at Pensacola Beach.

"Seen enough?" I finally asked Emily.

"Yeah. Let's continue."

I tossed my half-finished drink in a trash receptacle by the beach walkway and led the way back to the truck. I pulled around the horseshoe and hung a left, continuing southeast on 30A, which hugged the shore for 30 more miles. When we reached Rosemary Beach, I turned to Emily. "Do you want to stop?"

She looked out at the colorfully painted storefronts, the umbrella-shaded café tables, and the throngs of tourists. "Nah, that's okay. I'm cuteness-and-cupcaked out. I'd like to see an example of New Urbanism that's a smidge less cutesy sometime, if such a thing exists."

A few miles past Rosemary Beach, 30A picked up 98 again and widened back out to a four-lane road. Route 98/30 took us over a bridge and east through Panama City before curving sharply to the south. After a couple southbound miles I took a left onto Route 22, also known as the Wewa Highway.

The Wewa Highway was a two-laner. "Wetlands!" Emily said, looking out the window as we passed through a marsh. "This looks promising. Maybe there's some actual mitigating going on here after all."

We traveled the entire 24 miles to Wewahitchka, the eastern terminus of Route 22, without seeing another vehicle.

"Eerie," I said as I eased to a stop at the end of the road. Route 22 T-ed into Route 71, another two-laner. There was a Chevron station across the road from us with a van in the parking lot. Nobody came in or out of the convenience store. The gas pumps were all deserted.

"Maybe the world ended, and everyone forgot to tell us," Emily said.

The light turned green. "Which way do I go?"

"Make a left. The mitigation bank is north of here."

I turned. We passed a McDonald's, which was open, and the Red Roof BBQ, which was boarded up. "Sign of the times," I sighed. Keith used to rave about the Red Roof, but somehow I had never made it over here with him. Now I would never have the experience.

We passed signs for Lanier and Sons and the Smiley Apiaries, two of the most famous tupelo honey producers. Then Wewahitchka was behind us. Once more we traveled through acres of woody wetlands. "It shouldn't be much farther," Emily said. "The bank is supposed to be on the south side of Dead Lakes." I drove another mile. "There!" Emily said, pointing to a turnoff on our right. "Jehu Road's the address on the website."

I made the turn onto Jehu. We rode for a couple of miles, glimpsing an occasional house through the trees. Finally on the right I saw another one of the unobtrusive Mitigation Solutions signs beside a dirt road.

We bounced along for half a mile past pine and oak trees,

then came to a place where the road was covered with a puddle about 10 feet across. I gunned the engine and went for it. But the puddle was deeper than I expected. Halfway through we lurched to a stop.

"Melissa Joan Hart."

Em looked at me with big round eyes. "Don't worry, I've got this." I shifted the truck into four-wheel drive, then slowly hit the gas. I felt the tires start to grip and the truck moved forward a little, though at the same time, it sank deeper into the mud in front of it.

"No good." I shifted into reverse and hit the gas. The truck worked itself out of the mud, then suddenly shot backward out of the puddle. I turned the engine off. "I think we'd better walk from here. We'd probably be fine, but I don't want to risk it."

"Agreed," Emily said, unlocking her door and scrambling out of the truck. I set the emergency brake and pocketed the keys, then joined Emily, who was standing at the edge of the puddle looking ruefully back and forth between it and her ballet flats. "Not to worry," I assured her. I walked back to the truck bed and removed a pair of hip waders, which I pulled on over my tennies.

"That's great for you, but what about—oh!" I scooped her up and carried her across the puddle. At its deepest it was over my knees, but never high enough to spill into the waders. I walked deliberately, not wanting to lose my balance and dump Emily into the water. Or myself, for that matter.

"You're really strong," Em marveled.

I grinned at her. "You're light as a feather." I reached the other side and set her down. The ground was muddy but firm. "I guess I'll keep these on, until we see what lies ahead."

We continued down the path. The trees thinned out, so there were patches of bog visible between them. Palmettos and shrubby oaks grew there, as well as some stubby-looking trees covered with small red fruits.

"Are those crabapples?"

"Mayhaw," Emily said.

"Mayhaw?"

"That's right, mayhaw. How do you think they make mayhaw jelly?"

"Oh yeah. One of my roommates in college was always bringing that stuff back after weekends at home and trying to get me to put it on my toast."

"Did you?"

"Once. It was kind of sour. I'll stick with peanut butter."

The road ended in a clearing spreading up to the north, where a good-sized lake was visible. The ground between us and it looked solid, but I knew better. Probably full of sinkholes. Snakes, too. "What do you think?"

"Mayhaw, tupelo, spider lily," Emily said, pointing to a couple of trees near the lake's edge with trunks that flared at the bottom and to a cluster of plants about knee high, with tall blade-like leaves and white flowers that did indeed look spidery. "This is definitely freshwater wetlands."

"Well okay, then. Score one for Mr. Deaver. Time to head to Port St. Joe and get drunk."

Port St. Joe was 25 miles directly south of us. Only in the final few miles did we start seeing other vehicles again, mostly trucks pulling boats back home after a day out on the water. We stayed on 71 until it intersected 98. There, a block from Saint Joseph Bay, was the Port Inn. I pulled into the parking lot.

I awoke to the sound of Emily snoring on her side of the king-sized bed. I dragged myself to the bathroom to pee and splash some water on my face, threw my hair back in a ponytail, and tiptoed out of the room in search of coffee and juice. I had taken a glass of water and a couple of aspirin after our liquid evening, so I wasn't feeling too bad, but I didn't think Emily would be as fortunate.

However, before passing out in a Cosmo-induced stupor, Em had managed a worthy insight about Reclamation Acres. It was the end of the evening and she was rolling her martini glass back and forth against her forehead when she sat straight up and stared at me.

"What?"

She set her glass down. "Here's the thing. If the Gulf County mitigation bank is *already* wetlands, then how is it mitigating anything if a coastal developer pays Deaver for mitigation there?"

"Not sure I follow you."

"The idea of mitigation banks is that there's no net loss of wetlands acreage. A developer who wants to build on wetlands pays a mitigation bank to make sure that for every acre of wetlands he uses up, an acre of new wetlands will be produced elsewhere."

"Right."

"But if the acres in the mitigation bank were *already* wetlands, then there's no new wetlands produced by the mitigation bank. The new development still results in a net loss."

She had a point. "But maybe that's because Deaver has already reclaimed that land."

"Oh, c'mon. He hasn't done a thing to that land and you know it."

It was true. The land in Reclamation Acres had clearly been untouched. "You're right."

"And if *that's* the case," Emily was getting flushed with the effort of all this drunken thinking, "then what's the developer paying Deaver *for*?"

"That's the million-dollar question, isn't it?"

"Yup," Em said. Five minutes later, she was passed out in her

Adirondack chair on the Inn's porch; I'd had to carry her ass up to bed.

She'd been spot-on with her questions, though. It was hard to see how Deaver and the developers could be so blatantly scamming the Feds. The EPA had been hot on wetlands preservation for the past 25 years; the idea that they'd endorse a program with such a gaping loophole was crazy. But it was also hard to see how Deaver's mitigation bank was even pretending to do anything about wetlands loss. Even a drunken Emily could see that.

I said hey to the guy behind the desk as I crossed the lobby to the continental breakfast. I stuck a donut in my mouth and grabbed a cup carrier from the pile, then starting filling coffee and juice cups.

"Good morning," he said, looking up from his mobile. "Are you one of the guests from Gulf Breeze?"

"That's right. Why do you ask?"

"A guy crashed his plane there yesterday. Well in Santa Rosa County, anyhow. Some crazy developer trying to get out of his debts." He turned his mobile toward me. I walked closer. Staring up at me from the little screen was the face of Dan Bradford, scourge of Yellow Tree.

Half an hour later we were on the road. Em had looked a little green around the edges when she got up, but after coffee and aspirin and bacon and juice and more coffee, she was doing better. She was curled in the passenger seat with her feet tucked under her, sipping yet another cup of coffee. As we headed out of town, I told her about Bradford crashing his plane.

"Those people in Yellow Tree probably shot him down."

We arrived on the outskirts of Gulf Breeze a couple hours later. We were nearing the Garcon Point Bridge when I spotted The Chief's car in the turnoff lane. I picked up my cell and dialed his number.

He answered and said, "Don't tell me. You and Emily were arrested in Port St. Joe, and you want me to put in a good word for you with the local sheriff."

"Close. But I just flashed my Gulf Breeze PBA card at him and he sent a couple of his deputies over to wash my truck. Which was quite the job, since Emily had puked all over it."

"Ugh," Emily groaned as The Chief cracked up.

"Now I'm just wondering what's in Milton that could possibly take you away from Nancy's Sunday ham."

I pulled into the turn lane behind him. He looked up in his rearview and honked.

"Did you hear about Bradford?" he asked.

"Yeah."

"He took off into the woods after his plane crashed. We think we have a bead on him. Want to come watch?"

"Of course. Can we?"

"We don't know whether he's armed or not. He's clearly half off his rocker. Not a situation we'd ever want civilians to touch with a 10-foot pole. So sure, why not?"

"Awesome." I disconnected and explained the situation to Em. I was afraid she wouldn't be up for it, but her eyes brightened and she sat up straight.

"Robert Livingston Seagull, let's get that fucker," she said. Em had dealt with almost as many calls from disgruntled Yellow Tree residents as I had. She too bore Bradford a grudge.

I followed The Chief across the long sweep of the Garcon Point Bridge. Though not quite as long as the Three Mile Bridge, it was even more impressive, with a high, arching span that offered glorious views of the tranquil waters of East Bay and the pristine wetlands of north Santa Rosa County. "Bo's Folly," I said when we were halfway across.

"Huh?"

"This bridge. That's what they call it. Nicknamed for Bo Johnson, a state representative who went to prison for tax fraud in 1999, the year this thing was finished."

"It's only 10 years old?"

"Yup. They broke a speed record building it and got paid all sorts of bonuses. Then they were fined $4 million for violating the Clean Water Act."

"I hear they're raising the toll to $4."

"They keep raising it because the bond's coming due. But they'll never break even on this thing. They estimated toll revenue based on Okaloosa County, as though the bridge fed into Destin, with all its tourist traffic, and got a bond based on that. Instead, it feeds into . . . well, you know."

"The Gulf Breeze Costmart," Em said incredulously.

"That's right."

"Henry Wadsworth Longfellow! It's not even pointed at a beach! That's a fail of epic proportions."

"Yeah. Or not. You gotta assume Bo didn't really forget where the bridge was going. But someone really wanted to build it, and he made it happen for them. He must have had some pretty serious bribe money stashed away somewhere. He just got lazy and forgot to hide it properly, and that's how they got him on the tax evasion charges. IRS said he'd forgotten to report 'consulting fees.' And by the way, Jonathan Livingston Seagull is *not* a famous dead writer. Don't think I didn't notice."

We followed The Chief through the tollbooth, paid the outrageous toll, and continued north on 281.

Up ahead The Chief put on his right blinker and slowed down, then turned onto a dirt road. We watched the squad car bounce along ahead of us.

"He's going to blow out the shocks on that thing," Emily said. After about a quarter mile we came to a clearing.

"Molly Ringwald, will you look at that." In front of us, on the far side of the clearing, a small single-engine plane, painted a jaunty blue and white, dangled from the trees. The Chief pulled around to that side and got out. We did the same.

"So he crashed here?" Emily asked.

"The plane did."

"Huh?"

"He was flying from Destin to Peter Prince, the airfield up in Milton. It's a quick flight. Shouldn't have taken him much more than half an hour. About 20 minutes out he sent a distress call back to Destin, saying his windshield had imploded and he was 'bleeding like a stuck pig.' Then they lost contact. The FAA was putting together a rescue plan when a call came in from a fisherman over this way saying he saw a small plane go down. The fisherman was pretty sure no one was on board. The Milton sheriff's office sent someone out and this is what he found."

The Chief led us closer to the plane. The tail end was toward us but we circled around until we could see the front of the plane. It featured an intact windshield—and an open cockpit door.

"So he survived?"

"Assuming the fall didn't kill him. We think he parachuted out, then let the plane crash. Based on the fisherman's location, Chief Lemore thinks he circled around to the north before sending the signal and abandoning the plane. As you can see, it looks like it was headed south when it crashed, though the Destin-to-Milton flight plan would have him flying due northwest at this point. The Milton boys are putting together a manhunt north of here. I just need to wait for the crime-scene guys to get here and then we can join them. And there they are now."

As The Chief spoke a Ford SUV bounced into the clearing and came to a stop behind my truck. Two guys jumped out and started unloading equipment. It was the guys from Portofino

Beach who'd done the crime scene after Karen's kidnapping. They grinned at Em and me. "We have to stop meeting like this."

The Chief waved at them and headed back to his car, Em and I trailing him.

"You want to see the manhunt, don't you?" he asked.

"What do you think?"

CHAPTER FOURTEEN

Karen clasped her hands together, stretched her arms in front of her, and twisted until her knuckles cracked. Then she jerked her neck to one side and then the other. Crack, crack. She felt shriveled inside her own body. She would have liked to do a few yoga poses, then go for a 10-mile hike with Joe. It felt like it had been a year since she'd stretched her legs properly.

On the plus side, she'd just managed to finish an impassioned argument demonstrating the folly of destroying wetlands with the false promise of one day recreating others elsewhere that also happened to have the message KAREN IN MILTON hidden in it. Of course, she didn't really know for sure that she was in Milton, but some things Bud had said during the past two days left her feeling certain that she was somewhere in north Santa Rosa. Milton would at least give Joe and the police a place to start looking.

Assuming they ever got the message. This was her third letter. After her first letter, which she'd stretched out over two days, they'd settled into a letter-a-day routine, a pace her kidnapper seemed to find acceptable and which allowed her to play around with layout on the typewriter so her hidden messages would remain covert to the kidnapper's review. She trusted, however, that they would reveal themselves as soon as the printer started typesetting. But was there a printer? For the past two days, after reading her handiwork, Bud had sat at the typewriter himself to address the envelope to the *News Journal*, then journeyed out, presumably to the Post Office, though each time he'd tied her to the radiator in the living room—yes, the radiator—so thoroughly that she hadn't been able to free herself during his absences, which were brief. Therefore she assumed they weren't far from a post office, or at least from a drop box. She racked her memory for details about the postal situation in north Santa Rosa, hoping to come up with a nugget she could encode into her next letter, but so far she hadn't been able to remember any useful details.

Surely the first letter had been delivered by now. Surely the newspaper had decoded her message and alerted the authorities. Surely they'd begun tracing the envelope back to its point of origin. Surely they were out there, waiting for him to drop off the next letter, so they could follow him home and get her the fuck out of here.

She was quite sure none of the letters had been printed yet. Of course, it was unlikely they would be, since he insisted upon sending them via snail mail. She assumed that meant he feared having the letters traced back to him online.

Why was that? Had he tied himself to the mitigation banks publicly in some other way? Let it be known she wouldn't be released until the mitigation program was discontinued?

Was she to be the Martyr of Mitigation?

Karen tried to muster some enthusiasm for the idea of being the poster child for mitigation bank awareness, but she wasn't up to it. She just wanted to go home. She would continue the fight for wetlands there. After a very long nap. And some yoga. And a hike. And maybe a little primal scream therapy.

He entered the room. "How's it coming?" he asked. He was always deferential when it came to her writing. She supposed anything that reminded him of why he'd gone to all the trouble to kidnap her in the first place was a good thing. She'd begun to suspect that the reason so many kidnapping victims wind up dead is because it turns out to be such an anxiety-producing nuisance for the kidnappers to have a stranger around all the time. And even worse, one who serves as a constant reminder of the felony you've just committed. Much simpler to just commit one more felony and be done with the whole business, with nothing more complicated than a body to dispose of.

"I just finished," she said, handing him the letter.

He read through it slowly, his brow furrowing as he did so. His lips moved slightly as he read. On the day she finished her first letter he'd told her, without embarrassment, that he had big ideas but didn't read and write especially well.

"This sounds good," he said when he'd finished. "I like the way you use this House Bill 1349 as an example of the way state legislators and developers work together to take away wetlands protection."

"Thanks."

"I need to get this ready. You'll need to come out to the sitting room." Was it Karen's imagination or did he seem a little embarrassed as he said this?

"Can I stretch for a few minutes first? I feel like every muscle in my body is cramping."

"I guess." He seemed taken aback by the request, but not hostile about it. He bent and untied her legs, then backed away. Karen felt pins and needles start in her toes and work their way up her legs as she stood. She banged each of her feet on the floor a couple of times.

He stood to one side of the doorway, which Karen took to mean she was allowed to walk out to the living room on her own. She did so slowly, not wanting to startle him. She walked over toward the red couch, her familiar spot, and bent and touched her toes. Then, not able to stop herself any longer, she placed her head and hands on the floor and did a headstand, balancing her legs against the wall behind her. She felt the muscles in her lower back, calves and feet stretch and relax.

"What'd you do that for?"

"I need to wake my body up. It feels like it's been asleep for days. That car trunk of yours didn't do me any favors, you know. As you've already pointed out, I'm not as young as I used to be."

"You're not going to try something funny, are you?"

"What, from down here?" She looked up at him and laughed. He grinned sheepishly back.

"I didn't mean to make you uncomfortable, though. I'll come down." Better not to push her luck. She swung her legs back down to the ground and got into a crouch. From there she rolled her back and put her hands against the wall and her head down, stretching her neck and shoulders.

Finally, she slowly stood back up. "Okay, I'm ready," she said, turning away from the wall and back toward him. But he was no longer watching her. He was looking out the window. As she watched he limped quickly over to his easy chair, picked up his gun from the end table, crossed back to her in two strides, and put the gun to her temple.

CHAPTER FIFTEEN

I followed The Chief up 281. After several more miles, we came up to a City of Milton black and white pulled over to the side of the road. The Chief pulled up next to it and rolled down his passenger-side window. There were two men in the front seat of the car. The driver was in uniform, but the passenger wore street clothes. The Chief had a brief conversation with the driver, then rolled his window back up. The Milton car took a turnoff, and The Chief and I followed.

The road emptied into a clearing. Ahead of us the Milton squad car stopped. The Chief pulled alongside it once again. I followed suit and parked.

"Howdy," the Milton uniform said when Em and I had gotten out of the truck.

"What's this, Tad?" the guy in shirtsleeves asked, looking at us with alarm.

"This is the Gulf Breeze Planning & Zoning Department."

"And they're here why? This guy could be armed and dangerous. Lunatic set a plane on autopilot and left it to crash—it's lucky he hasn't killed someone already."

The Chief looked like that thought was just occurring to him as well. "Maybe you two should stay in the truck."

I smiled noncommittally. The Chief raised an eyebrow. I sighed and climbed back into the driver's seat, rolling down the window so I could continue to listen as Emily climbed back aboard as well.

"What's the situation?" The Chief asked the other guy. I assumed he was Milton's Chief.

"We don't really have anything solid yet. Otherwise I'd have more of my guys here. But after we got the call about the plane, Smitty here saw a guy with a backpack hiking north on 281. Not somebody familiar to him—and we tend to know all the regulars. The drunks, the crazies, the bridgewalkers, and whatnot. We thought if Bradford bailed on the plane nearby, it's possible it might be him."

"He was limping a little, you know?" Smitty said eagerly. "Like maybe he landed badly when he parachuted out of the plane."

"Let's not get ahead of ourselves," The Milton Chief said.

"Did anyone see him parachute in?" The Chief asked.

"No," Smitty said. "It's more a feeling I had than anything else. And I knew this road leads back to the old Jenkins property. The whole family's lived out here for generations. Whenever one of his kin got married, Old Man Jenkins would build another shack, or move a trailer in. Now most of them are dead or gone. There's still a few cousins out here but they're scattered apart, and there's a bunch of empty buildings. I figured he might be planning to hole up around here for a while."

"But how would he know about it?" I called over to them.

Smitty looked a little miffed. "He's a developer in this region, right? I figure he knows a lot about the undeveloped land around here."

"As a matter of fact we know he talked to the Jenkinses a few years ago about the possibility of putting a commercial project out here," The Milton Chief said. "Our Planning & Zoning Department confirmed it. He was talking about some kind of combination shopping center/fish camp, I think it was. Our planner found notes from the meeting in his files. So Bradford definitely knows about this place, Smitty's right about that."

"What's the plan, then?" The Chief asked.

"We thought we'd check out some of the abandoned buildings. Maybe see if we can find one of the Jenkins cousins to talk to."

"Sounds good," I said, climbing back down out of the truck. I was hoping The Chiefs had forgotten about banishing us womenfolk. But no. The Chief turned and pointed back at the cab, so I climbed back in as the three men headed up one of the paths that branched off the clearing.

"Are we really just going to sit here?" Emily asked.

"Oh Katie Holmes, of course not. We just have to wait for them to get out of sight."

"Then what?"

"I guess we'll go the other way. Smitty made it sound like there's trailers and shacks all over the place out here. We'll just go find one."

When the men had disappeared down their path Em and I got out of the truck and circled around a bit, trying to decide which path we should take. Finally, Emily noticed a turnoff about 50 feet down the path where the lawmen had headed. We decided to start there.

A few hundred feet after the fork, we came upon a house. It was a small wooden single-story structure that looked like it had been abandoned for about a hundred years. The roof had caved in, the porch was cracked and sagging, and the whole thing was covered with kudzu.

"It looks like a fairy tale house," Emily said, stepping carefully onto the porch. "Maybe Sleeping Beauty's napping inside." She brushed aside some kudzu and peered through a filthy window. "There's still a whole bunch of furniture in there. There's a couch and a rocker and a couple of little tables, and, I kid you not, a Whataburger ashtray."

I was about to reply when we were interrupted by the distant sound of a man's voice, shouting, followed by two gunshots.

Chapter Sixteen

At first Karen thought Bud had gone all psycho-rapist crazy on her after all. But then, though the pressure of the gun barrel against her temple made her afraid to move her head, she slid her eyes toward him and saw he wasn't looking at her at all. He was staring out the window again. She slid her eyes toward the window. Outside she saw three men, one of them in a police uniform, the other two obviously plainclothes cops, walking across the field toward the house. They walked unhurriedly, in conversation with each other, directly across the field. Their guns were not drawn.

Bud must have observed these things too because all of a sudden he grabbed Karen from behind and shoved a hand over her mouth, then pushed her across the room, away from the window and down the hall toward the bedrooms and her little letter-writing room. He hustled her into a bedroom she hadn't seen before, jerked open a dresser drawer, and pulled out a balled-up pair of socks, which he proceeded to shove in her mouth.

"Hey!" Karen said, but then the cotton made her gag a little. He pushed her up against the wall, then set the gun down and grabbed a roll of duct tape from on top of the dresser *Why was there duct tape on top of the dresser?* Holding her up against the wall with a hand at her neck, he tore a piece of tape off the roll using his other hand and his teeth. He stuck the tape over the socks, picked up the gun again, and glared at her.

Like this was her fault. Karen noticed he was panting pretty heavily from the excitement. That was interesting. Lungs not in such great shape.

There was a rap on the door. "Hello? Anybody home?" a voice called.

Bud pushed her back out of the room and into the study, where the ropes he used to tie her while she was wrote her letters were curled on top of the desk. He shoved her into the chair, pulled her arms behind the chair back and bound her to the chair, then quickly tied a knot behind her.

"Make a peep and you're dead," he said and dragged her chair behind him as he went to answer the door.

CHAPTER SEVENTEEN

Em and I tore through the woods to the next clearing, where we came upon another little house. This one was in better condition than the other, though not by much. The roof was intact, but it too had been overrun by kudzu.

We approached from the back. There was a tiny porch, with rails sagging and a few steps leading down from the kitchen door. We could hear voices coming from the front of the building.

I gestured to Emily that we should split up and round the house from both sides. I took the north side and sent Em around the south way. The front porches on these cottages tended to be placed off center a bit, to the left as one faced the building. I thought the action was more likely to be to the north.

I rounded the first corner without seeing anything, though the voices grew louder. I approached the front corner of the house slowly, flattening myself against the wall and shimmying forward. When I reached the corner I cautiously peeked an eye around.

The two Chiefs and Smitty stood on the weedy lawn—Section 3.607, I thought automatically, though of course the Gulf Breeze code didn't apply in Milton—facing the porch. The Milton Chief and Smitty flanked The Chief, and both had their guns drawn. The Chief stood in the middle, his hands out in a supplicating gesture, showing that he was unarmed.

Which wasn't true, of course. I knew for a fact he had a .38

special on his belt and a 9mm around his ankle.

But what the guy on the porch didn't know wouldn't hurt him. He was an old-looking geezer, kind of small and scrawny. He had hold of a petite woman tied to a chair in front of him and held a .22 to her temple.

A domestic dispute? No, I decided, looking at the woman's white hair, which was cut into a neat bob. She wore fashionable jeans and Tevas. *Karen.*

So she was still alive and appeared uninjured. No one else seemed to be injured, either, and no one was down. Therefore I assumed the gunfire had been a few warning shots fired over the bow, or maybe just potshots the kidnapper had sent in the two chiefs' direction to let them know he was serious.

I looked down at the other end of the building. I saw a dark spot that might be Emily's little head peeking around the building, but I couldn't be sure. My guess had been correct; I was much closer to the action than Emily. That was good.

As though reading my thoughts, The Chief spoke to the kidnapper. He said, "What can we do to meet your needs while keeping Karen safe?" Then he took a step closer to the porch.

"Y'all can get the hell off my property right now!" the man yelled. I couldn't help noticing that he was out of breath. He looked about three-quarters of the way toward a coronary. Karen looked scared but not panicked. Her eyes were roaming around. She was trying to figure a way out of the situation.

I slid back from the corner and started looking around on the ground. At first I didn't see anything I could use. I considered one of my shoes, slipping the left one off my foot and testing its shape and heft in my hand. But it wouldn't do.

Then I got lucky. About 20 feet from the side of the building I saw a row of flattened, rounded stones partially embedded in the dirt. They looked like they came from a river bed, and in fact they probably had, though who knew how long ago. They were a little smaller than hockey pucks and would have made great skipping stones.

I scurried over to the stones and grabbed one. It felt just right in my hand. Then, just for good measure, I picked up one more and stuck it in my pocket. It never hurt to be overprepared.

I returned to my position against the wall and slid out to the corner. I'd been afraid The Chief might see me and be thrown off his game. But if he had, he gave no sign of it.

"I can't rightly leave here without Karen," he was saying. "But I'd be happy to ask my colleagues to step off the property if it would make you more comfortable. Then you and I can talk, man to man."

I saw the kidnapper's hand start to move on his gun.

I don't think so, said a voice in my head.

It wasn't for nothing that I'd been pitcher for the 2006 NCAA Championship softball team. I hefted my river stone and winged it toward the base of the old man's skull.

CHAPTER EIGHTEEN

Karen picked at her lunch. Joe had fixed miso soup and vegetable tempura. It was one of her favorites, but she couldn't find her appetite. Plus Joe's new habit of waiting on her hand and foot made her want to scream. Every time he brought her a tray of food, it reminded her of Bud. Or Belie Jenkins, her abductor's real, proper name. She should just tell Joe, so he would stop. But she couldn't seem to bring herself to talk about it.

That was his name. Belie Jenkins. Chief Tobin of the Gulf Breeze Police Department had told her. After that young woman, that friend of Emily Wright, had taken the kidnapper down by chucking a rock at him, bedlam had broken out. Belie had pitched forward, knocking her off balance, but she managed to catch her balance before she fell. Not so Belie, who crashed to the porch. In a flash Karen found herself surrounded by the three cops, plus Emily Wright and a tall, strong-looking blond girl who kept grinning at her for some reason. Karen thought she looked insane, but she had to admit there was something about the girl's confidence that made her feel a little better.

Within three minutes Chief Tobin had whisked her down a dirt path and into his car. It was unmarked, but he popped a portable LED light onto the roof and sped her to the Gulf Breeze Hospital, with lights on but no siren. On the way he radioed the Gulf Breeze police station, telling them to pick up

Joe and bring him to the hospital as well.

"I'm fine," she said when he'd set the radio handset back in its bracket. "I don't need to go to the hospital. Call them back and tell them."

"It's just a precaution. We need to make sure you're not seriously injured."

"I'm *not*."

"With all due respect, Ms. Baretta, you don't know that. You've been cracked on the skull."

"What makes you say that?"

The Chief raised his hand and lightly touched the back of her head. Reaching up, Karen found a lump the size of a mockingbird egg. It must have been there for the past four days, and she hadn't even realized.

"Oh."

"Do you remember anything that happened at the beach?"

"Not really. He must have hit me from behind. When I came to I was in the trunk of his car. We'd already crossed both bridges by then."

"That must have been when it happened, then."

"Maybe."

Chief Tobin's eyebrow raised. "You mean to say he hit you again?"

"Yeah. I kicked him and ran away when he let me out of the trunk, but he caught up with me. Next thing I knew I woke up on the couch with the mother of all headaches."

This time he whistled. "So, you took two blows to the head last Wednesday. You're lucky you're still talking. Let alone writing acrostics."

Karen felt a shiver of something run through her. Not quite happiness, maybe, but a deep satisfaction. "You saw my message then?"

He smiled grimly. "I saw both of them."

Three, she'd thought to herself, but it seemed mulish to say it.

True to his word, Chief Tobin had gotten her in and out of the hospital quickly. He'd whisked her straight past the ER waiting room and back into an empty curtained area. Almost immediately a doctor had appeared, done a quick exam, and then sent her up to imaging for an MRI of her head.

"I don't think this is necessary," she said again, but Chief Tobin and the doctor ignored her.

By the time she got back to her curtained area, Joe was there. Shortly after that, she was released.

A few hours later, Chief Tobin paid them a visit at home. To see how they were holding up, he said, and also to fill them in on what was known thus far. That's when she learned her kidnapper's name, Belie Jenkins. He was a member of the Jenkins clan, an old Milton family who lived on several sprawling acres up in the woods where Karen had been found. Their numbers had dwindled in recent years, and several of the homesteads on the property had been abandoned.

Belie's motive for the kidnapping appeared to be just what he'd told Karen—he wanted a mouthpiece to give voice to his environmental concerns. However, Chief Tobin said, they were looking at all the angles.

Karen wasn't quite sure what that meant, but she let it pass. "Where is he now?" she asked.

"At the hospital. He's in a coma. Doctors aren't sure he'll come out."

Shortly after that The Chief had taken his leave. Karen found his visit soothing. She'd gone to bed as soon as he left and managed to sleep through the night.

Monday morning is when her troubles began. She felt restless and irritable. She knew it was the aftermath of the trauma, and that she should try to take care of herself so PTSD didn't set in. Talk therapy. Meditation. Yoga. Long walks on the beach. Patience. Time.

The problem was, she didn't feel like giving herself time, or doing yoga. She felt like punching someone in the face. It wasn't Joe's fault that whenever he came too close, with a solicitous look on his face and another fucking bowl of soup, she felt like punching *him*. She knew he wasn't the person she really wanted to punch. That was just displacement.

Weirdly, though, it didn't seem like Belie Jenkins was the person she wanted to punch, either.

CHAPTER NINETEEN

For a long time afterward, The Chief gave me a hard time about that throw. If I were a member of his force, he said, he would have no choice but to put me on administrative leave, and he might not be able to save my job afterward. It had been too risky, letting loose like that when Karen was still a hostage. With a gun to her head, no less.

In response, I gave The Chief a hard time about the crucial information he'd withheld. Okay, so I wasn't a member of his force, and therefore wasn't entitled to any information, crucial or not. Nonetheless, precedent had been set, and I thought it was bad form of The Chief to hold out on me.

It turned out the kidnapper's name was Belie Jenkins, and it turned out his purpose in kidnapping Karen had been to make her write letters to the editor about the evils of mitigation banks. And it turned out Karen *had* written such letters, and the *News Journal* had delivered the first of them to The Chief, who had been in possession of it on the Friday before we found Karen.

Once it became clear no ransom demand was forthcoming, The Chief's suspicions had turned to the "Mitagate" sign from the Seashore parking lot, and the sad symbolism of the dead loggerhead. He reached out to his contacts in the local media outlets and asked them to alert him immediately if they received any anonymous tips, letters, or calls about mitigation banking, wetlands, or loggerhead turtles. Unbeknownst even to Emily, he'd interviewed all the other members of Panhandlers for

Change, too.

On Friday he'd received a call from Mark Schneider, the *News Journal*'s Executive Editor, after the afternoon mail had been opened and Karen's first letter was found among its contents. The letter—which had been typewritten on a manual typewriter, had no signature, and was mailed in a typewritten envelope with a Milton postmark but no return address—was typical of the fare *PNJ* received from the north Santa Rosa community. It was unusual only because it was spelled and punctuated perfectly, thanks to Karen.

The *News Journal* staff wouldn't have given the letter much thought, and in fact might have considered printing an excerpt, if it weren't for the phone call they'd received from The Chief the day before. As it was, Schneider called The Chief as soon as his assistant brought the letter to his attention.

"What do you want me to do?" the editor asked. "Should I run it?"

"Not yet. I'll send a car over to pick it up. We're going to need to trace it. You can make a copy if you need to, for your records. In the meantime, I need you to fax it to me."

Almost immediately, The Chief had spotted Karen's secret message. He'd always been good at word puzzles. In that first letter she'd simply spelled out her name, using the first letter of alternating words. She'd hidden KAREN in the first paragraph and BARETTA in the second.

Over the weekend The Chief had been working with the local Post Office to retrace the letter's path through their system when, in pursuit of Dan Bradford, we'd stumbled upon Karen and her kidnapper instead, entirely by accident.

"But all's well that ends well, right?" The Chief said, smiling wryly at me. It was Monday morning and we were gathered in the front office, clustered around Emily and Rosario's workstations to rehash the prior day's events. Mike, David, and Patrick had also joined us to hear the scoop firsthand.

The Chief was being sarcastic. All had not ended, and all had certainly not ended well. Belie Jenkins had slipped into a coma after I'd beaned him with that rock. Even now he was in the ICU over at Gulf Breeze Hospital, where staff had told The Chief he was unlikely to wake up.

Everyone seemed to imagine this news would upset me. "Look, I didn't tell him to kidnap Karen and put a gun to her head," I told Emily, a tad snappishly, when I got tired of her solicitousness. "I would never have made it into a win–lose situation. But since he did, I have no problem with him being the one who loses."

In fact, my feelings about Belie were a little more complicated than that, but I was suppressing them for the time being. That was probably the reason I was giving The Chief such a hard time about Karen's letter to the editor. Trying to focus everyone's attention away from me.

It worked, inasmuch as I succeeded in irritating The Chief. "She's turning into my work wife," he complained to Mike. "Isn't she supposed to be *your* work wife?"

"Emily is Mike's work wife," Rosario said. And it was true. Em fussed over Mike like a mother hen. She fixed his lunch, nagged him about staying at the office too late, and jealously guarded his appointment schedule.

Once we'd rehashed everything a few times, Patrick said something about having a city to run and headed over to the main building. The rest of us took that as a hint and the party broke up. "After you're settled in, come talk to me," Mike said as I headed for my office. "Emily, you'd better come, too."

Uh oh, I thought. Maybe this time I'd finally overstepped my bounds. It *was* kind of crazy how much Mike and The Chief let me get away with—even I realized that.

I tossed my purse in a drawer, checked for messages, then went across the hall to Mike's office. In the hallway I met Emily, wearing her worried look.

"Have a seat, and please close the door." As we did so, I began mentally mounting our defense. We'd gone to the Jenkins property on our own time. We'd been off the clock. Etc.

But it turned out none of it was needed. Ahab was back on his usual obsession. As soon as the door was shut, he announced, "I had a tip this morning about the GulfBreezeSingles signs. I didn't want Rosario to hear until we have our ducks in a row."

I glanced over and saw Emily's brow relax as Mike picked up a piece of paper on which he'd written some notes. "The tip came from a Mrs. Mascione. She called me first thing this morning. She was having trouble sleeping last night so she went out for a walk. She said she was wearing her slippers so she was very quiet. Also, there was heavy cloud cover, and it was only a quarter moon last night anyway, so things were pretty dark."

"Oh my gosh, get on with it already!"

But Mike was enjoying himself. "Hey, these are the notes she gave me—this is her level of excruciating detail—so I wanted to pass them on to you verbatim. One never knows what will jump out as significant to two amateur detectives such as yourselves."

"What's jumping out as significant is how long it's taking for you to tell this story," I groaned. "The Internet will be obsolete by the time you're finished. There won't be any reason for the GulfBreezeSingles website to exist anymore. Our sign problem will take care of itself."

"Mrs. Mascione is that older lady who lives behind Bruno's. You remember her, right?" Mike continued, ignoring my sarcasm. "You took some calls from her last year."

"How could I forget?"

"What?" Emily asked. The Mrs. Mascione incident had been

before her time.

"Mrs. Mascione felt we were overwatering Shoreline Park last spring," I explained. "She thought it was wasteful. She called Rosario every day for three weeks. Then she called the Mayor. Then she collected water from the park sprinklers in a saucepot and called the media. She told them we were watering the park at the equivalent of six inches of rain per hour."

"Were we?"

"Sort of," I admitted. "So, she's friends with us again?" I asked Mike.

"She's on our side when it comes to the dating signs."

"So? What's her story? Do you think you could get to the point sometime this century?"

"It was a dark, cloudy night. Wearing her slippers and her deceased husband's black bathrobe, Mrs. Mascione stepped out for a late-night constitutional. As she rounded the corner by the post office, she saw a man planting a sign in the median in front of the bank. She hid behind an azalea bush and watched him."

"She can't have seen much," I objected. "If she kept telling you how dark it was. Anyway she's got to be like 150 by now. She's probably blind as a bat."

"This is what she saw," Mike said. "She saw a man, around 5' 8″ in height, a little bow-legged. A 'bandy rooster,' she called him. He stuck the sign in the ground. Then he pulled it out and replanted it—evidently he didn't like the angle the first time. Then he got into a tan Ford Ranger and drove away."

"Sarah Michelle Gellar!" I exclaimed.

"See anything?" Emily asked. It was just before two a.m., making it approximately 23 hours since Mrs. Mascione had seen the sign suspect in action.

"Same old same old." I was in the driver's seat of the parked F-150. We were surveilling the spot where we thought the suspect was most likely to appear, using infrared binoculars we'd borrowed from The Chief. I had them trained on a car parked half a block away. It had pulled up in front of one of the street's modest houses 10 minutes ago. Now the windows were fogging up. "Babies making babies."

"Any sign of the *suspect*?"

I directed the binocs back to a house located two down from the make out car. "Not a thing. Wait, I may have spoken too soon." The front door of the house opened and a cat emerged. A moment later, a man stepped out of the house and crossed the lawn behind the cat. He went into the garage, which was open, and put something into the bed of the truck that was parked there, an older Ford Ranger. I couldn't quite make out what, as the truck was partially backed into the garage. But I thought I could guess.

The man got into the Ranger and drove off. I set down the binoculars and took off after him, hanging back until he'd made a left and moved out of sight. Then I accelerated, tapping the horn as we rode past the car with the groping teenagers. They jumped apart as our truck passed.

"That wasn't nice," Emily said. "Interrupting their ardor."

"I did them a favor. He wasn't using a condom."

"Maybe she's on the Pill."

"Oh, honey. You're not from around these parts, are you?"

I was pretty sure we were headed back out to the 98 so I hung back until I saw the Ranger turn onto the highway a couple blocks ahead of us. Then I sped up again. The Ranger had already pulled ahead quite a bit by the time we joined it on 98.

"Doesn't look like he's headed to Bruno's," Emily said in surprise as the Ranger buzzed by the darkened supermarket without slowing.

"I think he's going to Costmart this time. That's been the

150

usual rotation."

"I didn't know there was a usual rotation."

"Oh yeah. I know Mike doesn't think so, but I *have* been paying attention to what this sign guy's been up to."

A couple miles later the Ranger did indeed slow at the stop light for the Costmart shopping center. I was still a quarter mile back, so I ducked into a strip mall a block before the big-box stores. I wound around the back of the buildings, crossed a side street, and drove behind the Costmart complex, emerging into the front lot on the far side of Lowe's.

The Ford was parked toward the front of the lot, not far from 98, next to an island with a dinky little tree planted in the middle. I turned off my headlights and inched toward the front of the lot. Emily took the binoculars off the bench seat between us and peered out through them.

"He's taking a sign out of the truck bed," she reported. "He's walking toward 98. He's planting the sign! Right there in front of everyone! He's not even being sneaky about it."

"First of all, there is no *everyone* out and about in Gulf Breeze at two in the morning. There's only us, and normally even we wouldn't be here. Second, *of course* he just walked up and did it. That's what people do when they're doing something wrong. Didn't you ever sneak into a club when you were underage? Or shoplift?"

"Not really." Emily looked regretful at the thought of her wasted, law-abiding youth.

I accelerated past the Ranger and flipped my headlights on. The sign guy froze in their glare. I rolled down my window and leaned out.

"Hey, Shawn. What's up?"

The next day I rolled into the office around nine a.m. I felt that catching Shawn red-handed in the act of planting a GulfBreeze-

Singles sign at two a.m., thereby ending four months' worth of angina for Captain Ahab, warranted an extra hour of sleep that morning.

When I got in, they were all abuzz about it. Mike alternated between indignation that the perpetrator had been under our noses the whole time and glee that he'd finally been caught.

"I just can't believe it," Rosario was saying as I walked through the door. "I can't believe he would do that!"

"It makes sense, though, when you think about it," I said. "He was getting money from the dating service for putting the signs out and from us for taking them down. What could be better? It probably meant he had to make fewer of them. He could just recycle some of the ones he picked up while doing code enforcement."

"I guess," Rosario said, looking troubled that there was such duplicity in the world.

"Are you saying you were on to him all along? That you knew our sign guy was *the* sign guy?" David asked. He was sitting at one of the guest tables in the visitor area, redlining the Jessica Biel out of some poor developer's engineering drawings.

"No," I admitted. "I didn't have a clue. But I got to thinking about it last night after The Chief hauled him off, and I realized it made perfect sense. We should have been looking at Shawn all along."

"We'll have to remember that in the future," Mike said.

As Mike, David, and I headed back to our offices, Emily scootched behind me. "Lunch today?"

"Sorry. I already have plans."

My plans involved another trip to the hospital, which I approached even less enthusiastically than when we'd visited Joe. But it was something I had to do.

When I arrived I stopped at the Information Desk, then rode

the elevator to the fourth floor, looking for the room number they'd given me. At the entrance to room 411, I paused.

The patient wasn't alone. An elderly woman sat in a chair beside his bed. She was tiny and wrinkled, but her posture was straight and her iron gray curls looked like they'd just come out of a wash and set that morning. She wore a flowered housecoat and gold-rimmed bifocals. Her hands were folded quietly in her lap. She appeared to be dozing off.

Behind her a man leaned into the window well. He looked to be in his early 60s. He was wearing jeans, a plaid shirt, and a belt with a huge metal buckle depicting a 12-point buck. He held a Styrofoam cup in one hand. As I watched, he spit discreetly into it.

I stepped into the room. "You from the Social Work office?" the man asked.

"No. I just came to see Belie."

"I didn't think he knew any girls," the man said. "At least, not any pretty ones."

"You're the one done did it," a voice intoned. I felt a shock run up my spine. The old lady's eyes had opened, and she was staring right at me.

I quickly weighed my options. "Yes."

I was prepared for an outburst, but the old woman just continued to stare. "I'm sorry," I said, though the woman's stare held no hostility. I stole a glance at the tobacco-chewing man. He too was looking at me calmly.

"What's done is done," the woman finally said. "Belie shouldn't ought to have messed with that woman."

"He didn't *mess* with her, Ma," the man said.

"You don't call it messin' to crack a woman on her skull and drag her off against her will?"

"I'm not saying what he done was right. I'm just sayin' he didn't mess with her. You know. In a sexual manner."

The man spit into his cup again as he said this and looked at me.

"The doctor says his brain is gone," the old woman said. "We told them it was okay to unhook him from all these machines, but they said we have to talk to someone from Social Services first. I'm his Aunt June. I'm his closest kin since his mama passed. After that they'll unhook him, and then he'll die."

"Maybe not right away, though," the man said. "They said it might take a day or two."

"I'm sorry," I said again.

"Belie weren't ever quite right after Korea," the man said. "Maybe not even before that."

"Now Eddie," the woman said. "Y'all got along like two peas in a pod when you were boys."

"There was still something strange about him, though," Eddie said. "Especially when he developed that fixation on the swamp."

CHAPTER TWENTY

The only time Belie Jenkins ever left Santa Rosa County was a four-year stint in the Army when he was 18. They'd sent him to South Korea where, he told his cousin Eddie when he got back, it was cold enough to freeze the balls off a brass monkey. He spent 18 months in Korea and swore he was cold the whole time. When he got home he vowed he would never go anyplace cold again.

Evidently that meant never leaving home at all. He returned to the Jenkins homestead and set up a little trailer in one corner of the family complex. According to the cousins, Belie's home had been unadorned but neat. Clean even, unlike the abodes of some of their other relatives, who got the packrat gene bad. Once he was resettled in Milton, he hunted, fished, and repaired the occasional wooden pallet to make propane money for his generator. And that was about it.

The decades rolled by. He was attentive to his mother, bringing her catfish or rabbits that he'd cleaned and dressed, and making himself available to help her with chores around the house. After she died he abandoned his trailer and moved back into her house, which had been his boyhood home.

The cousins felt that after Korea Belie "wasn't right," though an outsider might be hard pressed to understand what distinction they were making, in a clan full of not right. They might have been referring to the fact that Belie had chased girls a little before Korea, but never after. Or that he seemed more susceptible to, or at least more tolerant of, the womenfolk's religious carrying-on than other Jenkins men, accompanying his mother to church on Sundays long past the age of 12, which was when most male Jenkins abandoned the practice.

And then, sometime between Korea and the kidnapping, Belie developed a stronger than normal affinity for the swamp. All of the Jenkins relied on the swamp and felt at home there, but Belie took things even further. He started using terms like "wetlands" and "conservation." He was particularly passionate about freshwater wetlands. This was a reflection of the difference between north and south Santa Rosa. To the south were tourists and snowbirds, fancy hotels and overpriced drinks. The south was the Salt Life, which was a bit too cosmopolitan for residents of the northern part of the county. To the north it was not the gulf but the Blackwater River that formed the imaginative center of life. River families had their own version of the Salt Life. "Work sucks," a t-shirt popular in north Santa Rosa read. "I'm going to the river."

The Blackwater rose up in southern Alabama and wandered through Okaloosa and Santa Rosa Counties before emptying into a finger of Pensacola Bay called Blackwater Bay. Okaloosa County was named for the river; in Choctaw "oka" is water and "lusa" is black. The water was highly acidic and full of tannins, giving it the dark, transparent color of strong tea. And yet, like the gulf to the south, the river featured beaches of bright white sand. The contrast between the black water and the white sand was pleasing to the eye.

So Belie was a riparian wetlands champion, though all types of wetlands concerned and interested him. This was first brought to the clan's attention on the occasion of Aunt June's 80th birthday.

When asked what she wanted to do for her birthday, Aunt June had announced she wanted to visit the beaches of Fort

Pickens, as she hadn't since she was a teenager.

The clan didn't want to go to Fort Pickens. A trip to Fort Pickens meant driving more than an hour, crossing two toll bridges plus paying a third toll on Fort Pickens Road, and then having to sit on a beach where there was no shade but what you brought yourself. And once you got there, any sort of people might sit on the sand right next to you, and there wasn't much you could do about it. A beach full of strangers that weren't kin was not the Jenkinses' idea of a good time.

The Jenkinses weren't big fans of Fort Pickens itself, either. It was an interesting enough old ruin, if you went for that sort of thing. But Pickens had been occupied by Lieutenant Adam J. Slemmer, U.S. Army, in 1861, and held by him and 80 of his men throughout the Civil War, despite several Confederate attempts to take it.

As far as the Jenkinses were concerned, this lessened its value considerably. And they would have sworn Auntie felt the same way. But she was lost in some fantasy daydream from her youth, when she was young and beautiful and danced on the beach with a handsome boy in a uniform who'd taken her up in the dunes and had his way with her before shipping out and disappearing from her life forever. This fact had been a source of both shame and sorrow in her life for decades, but now, suddenly, on the eve of her 80th birthday, her shame was washed away, and she wished to return to the scene of the crime.

When one of the female cousins suggested maybe a barbeque along the river would suit her better, Auntie grew uncharacteristically snappish and said what did they ask her for then, if they were just going to do what they wanted anyway.

So off they went. They packed rafts and inner tubes and towels and chairs and homemade shade tarps, devised of large sheets of canvas and four fishing poles; and extra fishing poles, though none of them cared for the idea of gulf fishing much;

and coolers full of sandwiches and beer and gallon jugs of tea and toys for the few kids the family had managed to produce in the past 10 years. After decades of fecundity, the family was drying up.

They loaded all this stuff, plus the kids and the dogs, into three pickups and an ancient Lincoln Town Car that no longer shifted into fourth gear, and headed south.

Dogs weren't allowed on the beaches, but the Jenkinses would be damned if they let that stop them.

When they arrived they were relieved to see that the Fort Pickens beaches were fairly deserted. It was late August, getting to be the off season, and Fort Pickens was a long drive past the main Pensacola Beach tourist area, Casino Beach, which most of the remaining tourists seemed to find perfectly adequate for their needs.

They unloaded the pickups. Then the men unfolded their camp chairs and sat in a crooked row drinking beer while the women made their makeshift canopy, spread towels and blankets, and set out food on an ancient card table they'd brought for the purpose.

Back at home the card table wobbled, but it was perfectly stable in the sand.

True to form, Belie stayed on his feet to help the ladies, specifically his mother, who was still alive when the Fort Pickens excursion occurred. Mary had him squirting catsup onto hamburger buns when Cousin Eddie went back up the beach and tugged on one of the tall grasses that grew sparsely over the dunes. He intended to use it as a prop in some prank against one of the other cousins, but he never got that far. All of a sudden Belie was in his face, pointing the catsup bottle toward him menacingly.

"What's your problem?" Cousin Eddie asked. He was not inclined to be tolerant of Belie's eccentricities.

"That there's sea oats. It's a protected species."

"What are you going to do, turn me in to the Feds?" Eddie snorted, tugging on the stem some more.

"Sea oats prevent dune erosion," Belie said fiercely. "Take your paws off it."

His cousin stared at Belie in astonishment. *Dune erosion?*

He did it, though. He took his paws off.

CHAPTER TWENTY-ONE

When I got back to the office, I filled Emily in on how I'd spent my lunch hour.

"Sorry about not telling you where I was going earlier. I just felt like it was something I had to do alone."

"I understand. Do you feel any better now?"

"I'm not sure. It was a relief that his relatives weren't angry at me, but it was also disconcerting. Like, maybe if they'd been mad, I could have tried to win their forgiveness, and that would have given me some closure. Also, the more they told me about Belie, the more I liked him. Is it possible for me to have Stockholm Syndrome when I wasn't even the one he kidnapped?"

"I think you should talk to Karen," Emily said. "Joe called while you were at lunch and wanted to know if we would come visit her sometime. He says she's eager to talk to you."

"Sounds good to me. How about tonight after work?"

"We can't tonight. We have a Planning Commission meeting."

It was a sign of how out of my mind Karen + Belie + Sign Guy had me that I'd completely forgotten about our biweekly Planning Commission meeting. Mike, Emily, and I all had to be there—Mike and I to present agenda items and answer questions from the commissioners, Emily to take the minutes. Patrick and David usually attended as well, sitting over on the left side of the room with Mike and me at the staff table, while Em sat right up on the dais with the commissioners.

The meetings were held at 6 p.m. While Em got the meeting room ready, I reviewed the night's agenda. I was responsible for presenting the Robinson subdivision, which was seeking final approval. It was just a little two-lotter, and the Commission was expected to recommend it to City Council without further discussion.

The hot item on the evening's agenda was the Master Plan.

The city's current Master Plan was 15 years old, meaning it was hopelessly out of date. Santa Rosa County's population had grown by 25,000 residents between 2000 and 2008, an 18 percent growth spurt that put it in the top 3 percent of counties nationwide for population growth. And most of that growth had occurred in the southern part of the county, in the Fairpoint Peninsula corridor that stretched from Gulf Breeze to Navarre.

This meant that Highway 98, which was the only through road that ran all the way from the Three Mile Bridge to Navarre, was seeing a lot more traffic than it had 10 or 15 years ago. Traffic lights had been added, but it was still almost impossible to cross the highway on foot for much of its length. Meaning, people literally had to get in their cars to drive across the street.

Now, maybe they would have anyway. But it's bad policy, from a city planner's point of view, to make driving short distances a *necessity,* and even worse to have a street that's impossible for pedestrians to cross safely. Therefore, when Mike sat down with the outside consultants who'd been hired to draft the new Master Plan, he talked a lot about the need to create viable alternate traffic corridors through Gulf Breeze, to take some of the pressure off 98, and, if humanly possible, to improve walkability.

The problem was there weren't a whole lot of places to send traffic because the city was surrounded by water on three sides and had the National Seashore, in the form of the Naval Oaks

Reservation, right in its middle. But the consultants had made the best of it. Their proposed Master Plan showed Soundview Trail, a collector road that currently ran along the Santa Rosa Sound on the south side of the peninsula, crossing through Shoreline Park and hooking up with Shoreline Drive near the city's southwestern tip. The proposal was for a three-lane minor arterial with bike lanes in both directions and some commercial zoning to the east of Shoreline Park. The idea was that residents of this part of the city could do some shopping and errands without having to cross 98.

To the north, the consultants were more ambitious. Their blueprint showed Northcliff Drive, which currently ran along Pensacola Bay on the north side of the peninsula for about 2,000 feet before dead-ending in a field, hooking up with Bay Cliffs Road and then curving back down toward 98, past Gulf Breeze Hospital. The hospital was the site of a nationally known orthopedic clinic, and there was already a plan in the works to build an IT complex next to it, so expanding Northcliff into a collector made sense.

The Northciff Drive proposal also called for an offshoot that would be pointed toward the National Seashore. Thus far the Seashore, which of course was controlled by the Feds, had forbidden additional road construction within the forest. But Mike had friends in the Park Service, and he believed that if the county continued to grow, eventually the Feds would relent and allow a new road to be constructed across the north side of the forest, where it was narrowest. The Northcliff Drive turnoff would allow the city to prepare for that eventuality. Mike dreamt of a northside road that would run all the way from the Three Mile Bridge to the turnoff for Garcon Point Bridge, which connected lower Santa Rosa County to the upper two-thirds. Such a road could break up the residential/commercial/residential zoning sandwich that Gulf Breeze had become and put mixed use back into play.

Here's the thing about Master Plans, though. Just because something is on a Master Plan doesn't mean it's ever going to happen. A city doesn't draw up a new Master Plan then run out and redo the city to make it match. For one thing, no city can afford that. Rather, the Master Plan reflects the City Planner's best ideas about what would be a good strategy to handle anticipated changes in the city.

The way a Master Plan comes to fruition is through private development. Once a new Master Plan is approved by the local governing body, anyone who submits an application to develop a parcel of land in that jurisdiction is directed to follow its specs.

So, there was no guarantee that Northcliff Drive would ever be developed as an alternative route to 98. It might be drawn that way on the new Master Plan, and the new Master Plan might be approved and adopted, and it might be in place for the next 10, 15, or even 20 years. But if no developers came forward with proposals for that section of the city, the Northcliff Drive neighborhood would remain just what it was today: a sleepy mixture of waterfront mansions and little crackerbox houses with a road that dead-ended in a field.

That was the beauty of a Master Plan. It allowed growth and development to remain in sync. If no developers stepped forward, then the new Master Plan would change nothing.

However, during the two weeks since the last Planning Commission meeting, something had sent the Breezers into hysterics about the Master Plan. Some of the residents on the north side had somehow got it into their heads that the city was planning to come through their neighborhood with a bulldozer, tearing up their landscaping and their lawns, knocking down houses, if necessary, and squashing household pets in order to build a superhighway where drivers would earn points for mowing residents down, ala *Death Race 2000*.

At least, that was how the Breezers presented the situation when the calls started rolling in. They went to Emily's line first. Out of the blue one Tuesday morning she picked up the phone to find a hysterical woman on the other end, yelling about how the city was trying to sneak a Master Plan through without informing the public but they weren't going to get away with it because she, the caller, was onto them now. Furthermore, they couldn't just take the caller's yard to build their road. It was unconstitutional!

More calls poured in. Soon they started hitting my desk and Rosario's as well. My first caller insisted she wanted an audience with the Mayor. As soon as I was able to get off the phone, I headed into Mike's office.

"We have a problem."

"I know. I've been listening to you and Emily. What the hell's going on?"

"They think we're trying to sneak the Master Plan through without public input."

"We've been having meetings for a year! No one came!"

Mike was beside himself. He'd been scheduling public meetings about the new Master Plan for months, begging the public to show up and offer feedback. Most of the time he and the consultants would sit in the city meeting room alone for the allotted two hours. Sometimes I would show up with a bag of food from Whataburger, just because I felt sorry for them.

"They don't know what they're talking about," I assured him. "But something's got them all wound up all of a sudden. They think we want to build a highway in their front yards. The lady I talked to wanted to talk to the Mayor."

Mike consulted with Patrick, the City Manager, who consulted with Adam, the Mayor, who called Richard, the Chair of the Planning Commission, to ask if he would agree to a public session about the Master Plan at the next commission meeting.

Once Richard gave the okay, Mike went into overdrive. He called the consultants and asked them to make large blowups of the section of the proposed Master Plan that was causing all the uproar. Mike added a few posters of his own, including one with the definition of a Master Plan spelled out in letters two inches high, and another detailing the dates and times of all the meetings he'd scheduled about the Master Plan during the past year, where they'd been advertised, and how many people had attended.

Half an hour before the meeting was scheduled to start, Mike, David, Emily, and I stood in the meeting room, looking at Mike's posters and trying to help him find the optimal arrangement.

"I can't help thinking this is all a big linguistic misunderstanding," David said. "Like if only Master Plans were called 'Master Proposals,' or 'Master Suggestions,' we wouldn't be in this mess."

"That reminds me," Mike said, and he walked back down to David's office and ripped "The Creed of the Pavers" off the wall.

"Hey!" David said as Mike came back upstairs, tearing the Creed to shreds. "That was a personal item. Besides, we're not going to have an angry mob of Breezers carrying torches through our private offices, are we?"

Mike ignored him. "You'd better get that picture of Ms. Willis off your desktop, too," he said to me. I blushed as I headed down to my office to follow his order.

I was just shutting my computer down when David came into my office and slumped into the guest chair. "Mike tore down my 'Creed of the Pavers,' " he said mournfully.

"I know. He's just nervous about the meeting tonight."

"I should put 'The Creed of the Pavers' on one of his posters."

"Don't be naughty. You'll give him a heart attack."

Forty-five minutes later, I looked with amazement at the crowd that was jammed into the meeting room. By my rough count there were at least 100 Breezers present. The most I'd ever seen at a Planning Commission meeting was 25, and that was when one of the local Scout leaders had brought his whole troop at once to help them earn their Civics badge. A few of the latecomers sat against the wall on the side of the room opposite the staff table. The others stood in back.

Emily scurried to her place on the dais and opened her laptop.

Mike and David joined me at the staff table.

"Where's Patrick?" I whispered. The City Manager normally attended Commission Meetings. Mike shrugged, but David pointed toward the door, where Patrick had just entered the room, followed by the Mayor.

The Mayor did *not* normally attend Planning Commission meetings.

Richard Kaufman, the Planning Commission Chair, spoke. "Mr. Mayor. This is an unexpected pleasure." I suspected the pleasure wasn't unexpected at all, but the Mayor just grinned.

"Would you care to do the honors?" Richard asked, indicating his chair.

"No, no. That would be irregular. I'll just sit over here with Patrick and the others."

Patrick and the Mayor moved over to the staff table, and Richard banged his gavel. When the crowd had quieted down, he said, "Before we begin, I want to explain a few things about how this works, for those of you who might be joining us for the first time. The Planning Commission reviews all requests involving land use within the city limits, such as new subdivisions or rezoning requests. We also oversee and maintain the Development Code, with the help of our very able Community Development staff." He gestured toward us at the staff table.

"We make recommendations about these matters to City Council, which has the final say. There are two items on tonight's agenda. The first item is a request for final recommendation of approval for a two-lot subdivision. The Commission has looked at this project previously. Staff will make a brief presentation on the item, and then we'll open the floor to comments from the public, and then the Commissioners will *briefly* discuss it, and then we'll vote.

"Next we'll move on to the second item, the Master Plan, which I suspect is why most of you are here tonight. We're eager to hear your input about the Master Plan—in fact, staff has held several meetings about this Master Plan before tonight, and nobody came, so we're very glad to see y'all here now. The Commission isn't voting on the Master Plan tonight, so this will just be a discussion item. We're still going to follow some protocol, though. When we get to that item, once again the staff will make some introductory remarks, and then we'll open the floor to discussion from the public. I'll ask all of you to wait until the presentations are over before we start the discussion, and I'll ask everyone to conduct themselves with the manners and mutual respect I've come to expect from citizens of this fair town. That way we can make sure everyone has a chance to say their piece."

Richard paused and peered at the crowd over his glasses. "Are there any questions about procedure?"

You could have heard a pin drop. Richard was good at the whole authority thing.

"Very well, then. Our first order of business will be the Robinson subdivision, which is seeking a final recommendation of approval from this Commission. Ms. LaRue, can you walk us through this?"

★　★　★　★　★

Five hours later, my head hit the staff table. It was too heavy for me to hold up any longer. I rested it on my hands and watched the citizens as they argued with Richard, Patrick, Mike, the Mayor, and the consultants who'd worked on the Master Plan.

After five nonstop hours, the Breezers finally seemed to be running out of steam. That was the Mayor's plan, I knew; to give everyone a chance to talk until they'd just talked themselves out. It wasn't a bad strategy, in politics as in life. Sometimes it worked, sometimes it didn't.

Tonight it seemed to be working okay. Most of the citizens seemed mollified after dozens of reassurances that the city had no intention whatsoever of developing Northcliff Drive, or for that matter, any road. Rather, the staff—and Richard and the Mayor—explained, and then explained again, that the Master Plan only represented a possibility. Northcliff Drive *might* gradually be widened and expanded, on developers' dimes, if any developers were interested in coming in with new projects. Like Oriole Road, they added.

This had been a stroke of genius from Patrick, who'd sent Mike out 30 minutes before the meeting to take pictures of Oriole Road, which he'd then uploaded to his laptop and displayed using the projector.

Patrick kept them on display for the entire meeting. Oriole Road was an older Gulf Breeze through street. The oldest sections were only 16 feet wide, with no parking lane and no curb/gutter/sidewalk. The newer sections, which had been improved by three different residential developers, were 28 feet wide and had two lanes with a bike lane on each side, as well as curb/gutter/sidewalk. For years the city had received calls asking when it was going to improve the rest of Oriole Road to make it all like the new sections.

The images of Oriole Road, and the quiet persistence of

Patrick, Richard, and the Mayor, seemed to be having a positive effect. We'd gotten through the Robinson subdivision in about 15 minutes. The next hour and a half was taken up with a group discussion about the Master Plan. It started hot and then gradually cooled down. When it threatened to heat up again, Richard suggested the residents walk around the room and look at the posters. He positioned himself, the Mayor, Mike, me, and two of the friendlier commissioners at the posters. However, Mike had sputtered so much during his first few attempts to address questions that Patrick sent him back to the staff table and took his place, afraid Mike's indignation would only add fuel to the citizens' fire. When someone had a technical question, Patrick would direct them to Mike and the consultants for a quiet sidebar.

After the first hour David relieved me at my poster, allowing me to get off my feet. Now, two hours later, David too had returned to the table. The crowd of residents had thinned out considerably. The only holdouts who seemed to be hanging on to mistrust and rage were Phyllis Schenker and her father, Douglas.

Phyllis had been a few years ahead of me at Gulf Breeze High. She'd lived on the panhandle all her life. Her husband had run off last year, leaving her with three kids, the oldest of whom was six, the youngest, two.

You couldn't blame her for being pissed. But she seemed to have directed all the frustration from her personal life toward the Master Plan. She'd started a blog, "Save the Northcliff Neighborhood." On it she claimed the city planned to put a four-lane road through the bayside neighborhood, that Patrick was negotiating with the Feds to build a county jail in the National Seashore, and that Mike and Richard were in the back pocket of a developer who planned to put in a SuperTarget directly west of the Seashore. Needless to say, frequent, impassioned pleas to "think of the children" were included throughout this diatribe.

David had texted me a link to the blog about two hours into the meeting, and I'd read through it when I got back to the staff table. I tried to hide it from Mike, but it turned out he already knew. He was on his third reading of the blog when the meeting hit the five-hour mark.

"A SuperTarget wouldn't even *fit* in the Northcliff neighborhood," he muttered. "These people have no sense of scale."

"Some of the comments are reasonable," I said consolingly. "Like this person who says the city is just trying to plan for good growth, and that having an alternative road to the Three Mile Bridge is important for disaster preparation."

"Emily wrote that," Mike said glumly.

"Oh."

"Why do people always think I want to hurt their children? I care a lot about the safety of children! I'm trying to make Gulf Breeze *safer* for children!"

"I think those comments were directed more at her ex than at you," I said, looking over at Phyllis, who was still arguing with Richard. She'd been pretty in high school and grown up to be a striking woman. She had the most perfect eyebrows I'd even seen, amazing sweeping black arches. But now her hair had grown out into a nonstyle and seemed to be thinning alarmingly in a patch on the left side of her head. She was wearing a stretched-out, faded pink sweatsuit. Life was kicking her in the ass, and as a result she'd become a shlumpadinka.

Her father, Douglas, stood a few feet behind her. He was her partner in this battle, though I suspected his participation in "Save Northcliff" was more about a show of solidarity with his daughter than any real conviction that some long-shot commercial development on the north side of town signaled the start of End Times.

Watching him shuffle his feet as Phyllis continued to rant, I realized Douglas Schenker didn't look well. He was a little gray around the edges, and his hand clutched his belly. I texted David, even though he was sitting right beside me.

mr s looks ill

David looked up and his eyes found Douglas.

"Yeah, he does. I think this is more excitement than he's used to. That daughter of his should give it a rest and take him home."

A moment later, Douglas leaned in and whispered something to Phyllis, then turned and headed for the door. He walked with a shuffling gait, his hand still clutching his belly.

David and I watched him exit.

"Maybe we should go check on him."

"He'll be all right," David said, but then, a moment later, he rose out of his seat. "Fine, I'll do it," he grumbled. I grinned fondly at his receding back. However, he returned almost immediately.

"He's not out there. He must have headed home. I'm sure he'll be okay."

Just then Richard banged his gavel again. When everyone was settled, Richard thanked everyone for coming. He expressed hope that everyone had learned some things. Then, finally, he announced that the meeting was adjourned. It was 11:42 pm.

I thought everyone would rush out of the room immediately, but I was mistaken. People were still all jazzed up from the adrenaline rush of civic participation. They weren't ready to head home to bed just yet. They milled about, talking animatedly.

Emily zoomed around the room, collecting abandoned agendas and stacking chairs and cleaning up plates and cups. Once she had the room tidied, she could lock the door and head home, even if others wanted to linger.

I watched her packing up the laptop she'd used to take the minutes, her final move before heading out. Next to me at the staff table, David, Mike, and Patrick all sprawled in their chairs. Evidently they were too exhausted to think about leaving just yet. Though he looked dead on his feet as well, the Mayor was up again, circulating among the residents, smiling and bending down to hear what they had to say.

As I stared vacantly into the lingering crowd, I saw Phyllis Schenker take her phone out of her pocket and put it to her ear. She listened for a moment, then walked quickly toward the door.

I glanced over at David and saw that he'd noticed as well. But just then my phone vibrated where I'd left it on the table. I picked it up and looked at the screen. It was a text from Chris:

lonely w/o my baby

Immediately followed by a second message:

i have lasagna

"I'm out of here," I said to David. "Good night."

The next morning I arrived at the office to a minor uproar. Rosario was sitting at her workstation crying, while Mike and David stood at the counter, looking troubled.

I looked around in astonishment. "Who died?"

"Douglas Schenker," Mike said.

"Sarah Jessica Parker, I was just joking! What happened?"

"Last night at the end of the meeting he told Phyllis he wasn't feeling well and was going home," David said. "You remember—we noticed him leaving. He thought he had indigestion. He made it home and took some antacid, but it didn't help. By the time Phyllis got home he realized he was in trouble, and he asked her to call an ambulance, but when they got there, it was too late."

"Damn." It seemed like a situation where real expletives were called for.

I went around the counter and bent to give Rosario a hug in her chair, then walked back to my office and threw my purse on my desk. I was about to return to the reception area and join the wake when I heard a racket coming from the kitchen.

I headed farther down the hall and poked my head into the tiny room. Emily was standing in front of the open refrigerator door, chucking condiment bottles, salad dressing, and other items rather violently into a large trash bag she held in front of her.

"July 2007," she said, glancing at the label on a jar of mayonnaise before flinging it into the bag. "That thing expired a year before I started working here."

"What's up?" I asked.

Emily flinched. "Just cleaning out this refrigerator. No one here throws out anything that's expired, *ever.*"

"Oh. Well, that's nice of you."

"Look," Emily said, dropping the bag of condiment bottles to the floor with a loud clank and turning to the small round wooden table at the center of the room. It was there so we could take our lunch breaks in the kitchen if we wanted to, though none of us ever did.

Emily picked up a bottle of aspirin from the table and thrust it toward me.

It wasn't a name-brand bottle, and the lettering on the label looked distinctly old-timey.

"Dang, that looks old."

"It expired in 1999!" Emily exclaimed.

I still wasn't exactly sure why Em was so wound up. "Definitely not good," I said carefully. "I'll go at lunch and pick up a new bottle."

"These wouldn't have saved Douglas!"

"Probably not. But, Em . . . he didn't ask anybody for help. When he left, he thought it was just indigestion."

"But what if it were David—or Mike? They work themselves to death, they don't eat right . . . they're probably both on target to have their first heart attacks before 50."

Finally, I understood. I stepped over to the table and gave Emily a hug, then flung the ancient aspirin bottle into the garbage bag for her.

CHAPTER TWENTY-TWO

The more time that passed, the more Karen's sense of shame grew that she hadn't tried harder to escape. In retrospect, the kidnapper's frailty, his limp, the weakness of the restraints he used, the many possible routes she could have used to elude him, all seemed perfectly obvious.

Joe sensed this tendency in her and attempted to nip it in the bud. "You're *alive*," he insisted. "You're unharmed physically, and I hope more or less emotionally, too. He didn't attempt to rape you." (*He didn't, right?* he'd always repeat at this juncture, the vein in his right temple pulsing.) "He fed you and allowed you to sleep. If you'd tried to escape and he caught you he probably would have killed you. This is much better."

Karen appreciated the effort. But there was still a big corner of her mind that thought she'd betrayed herself in some fundamental way. She'd always imagined she was tougher. But when it came down to it, she hadn't acted because she'd been afraid of being hurt. That pain in her head on the first day had been excruciating, and she hadn't wanted more.

"Probably a concussion," Chief Tobin had said. "That's why you weren't more motivated to try and escape. Lethargy secondary to head trauma." He said it made it all the more impressive that she'd been able to compose the letters embedded with the secret messages.

Karen pretended to be mollified, but mentally she continued to beat herself up.

★ ★ ★ ★ ★

In an attempt to cheer her up, Joe had invited Emily Wright and Gail LaRue to dinner. Karen was eager to see them, but nervous. She didn't even know Gail, but she seemed to have developed strong feelings about her during the past three days— feelings that were all tied up with her feelings about Belie Jenkins.

On the one hand, she was glad Gail had taken quick action and gotten her out of his clutches. But she also found herself grieving the fact that Belie was likely to die soon. That's what Chief Tobin had said when he called on Monday: Belie would probably never come out of his coma.

She was astonished by how desolate the news made her. She realized she'd been counting on having at least one more conversation with Belie. A real conversation, with no guns. Where she could look him in the eye and ask what the hell he'd been thinking . . . and also, maybe, try to understand what it was about the mitigation banks that had made him throw away his life. Was it mitigation banks in general, or was there something in particular about the Eglin deal that made him nuts?

Belie. What the hell kind of name was that, anyway? The first few times she heard Chief Tobin say it, she assumed he was saying Billy, just with the funny accent they had down here. (Thirty years in the South, and she was still basically a Yankee.) Only when Chief Tobin emailed her a copy of his incident report did she see that she'd been spelling it wrong in her head.

His redneck upbringing belied his passion for wetlands conservation.

CHAPTER TWENTY-THREE

We'd only intended a short visit. We figured we'd run out there, spend a few minutes, then stop at Whataburger on our way back before going our separate ways for the evening. But when we arrived, it was clear they expected us to stay for dinner.

We agreed, but with some trepidation on my part. It turned out that Karen and Joe were vegans.

Here's a joke:

Q. How can you tell if someone is a vegan?
A. Don't worry. They'll tell you.

Joe went into the kitchen to finish preparing the meal while Emily and I sat in the living room with Karen. Their place was nice. It was a cozy little bungalow out in unincorporated Gulf Breeze, located at the end of a long street, right on the Sound. It was surrounded by pine trees. When Joe was giving us the tour he told us their neighbors, who lived in one of those frosted cake–type houses with a fiercely manicured lawn, were constantly getting on them to chop down the pines. The neighbors had moved in 20 years after Joe and Karen, and even though they'd been there for more than 10 years now, it was clear Joe still regarded them as interlopers.

I was sympathetic with the neighbors only inasmuch as it was all too easy to picture one of the trees sailing through the French doors of their house in a hurricane. However, if the stand of pines had made it through Dennis and Ivan, chances are it was solid.

"Did you lose any trees during the hurricanes?" I asked.

Joe gave me a funny look. "No."

The living room where we sat was weathered pine floors, sparse, square-cornered furniture, and walls lined with books.

Karen looked shaky.

"How are you doing?" Em asked her.

"Oh, you know. Okay, I guess." Her eyes flickered toward me, then she quickly looked away again.

"How's your head?" I asked. "The Chief said you were bonked pretty hard."

Karen's hand moved up to the back of her head, almost involuntarily. "Oh, it's okay. Better than the other guy's." Then, seeing my expression, she quickly added, "I'm sorry, that probably sounded really snarky. I'm very grateful for what you did."

"It's all right. I didn't start that fight."

"But you finished it. To tell the truth, I'm sort of embarrassed I didn't. He wasn't in such good shape, after all. But I did nothing. It kind of makes me want to punch someone."

"Like Belie Jenkins?" Emily asked.

"You'd think so, wouldn't you? But I can't seem to muster any anger toward Belie. Instead, all the indignation I've ever felt about how we handle wetlands conservation in this country has come back and hit me all at once, like a tidal wave."

Emily said, "In other words, you think Belie was right."

"Pretty much."

Em and I glanced at each other.

"If either one of you says the words 'Stockholm syndrome,' I'll smack you."

Joe came in to tell us dinner was ready. We moved into the dining room. The table was unstained birch and could seat six. There was a bench along one side and four chairs around the other three sides. I sat on the bench next to Emily and looked down at the plate Joe had set in front of me. One side of it was filled with crumbly brown stuff coated with a bright yellow sauce, sitting on top of something that looked like it wanted to be an English muffin. Vegan Eggs Benedict, Joe announced, saying he hoped we didn't mind having breakfast foods for dinner.

Yeah, like that was the problem. This is what I don't understand. Why would a vegan try to recreate Eggs Benedict? That seems like an exercise in unhappiness. If you want Eggs Benedict, why not just eat Eggs Benedict? And if you're vegan, eat something else.

The plate was rounded out with a cupful of nice-looking green salad and a small bowl of black beans. I started with a few mouthfuls of each of those before steeling myself to taste the vegan "eggs." But once I finally did, I was pleasantly surprised. Turned out they were delicious.

After we'd all eaten for a few minutes in silence, Joe put down his fork and looked at me. "I want to thank you for what you did," he said. "We're in your debt."

"No problem."

"I don't think you should feel bad about what happened to that man."

"Well. It is what it is." I looked over at Karen. "I went to see him yesterday."

"You did?"

"Yeah. His relatives were there. They were waiting to talk to a social worker, and then they were going to take him off life support."

"Were they hostile?"

"No, they were nice. They told me about a time when they were having a family picnic at the beach and Belie threatened his cousin with a catsup bottle because the cousin was pulling up a sea oat."

"Good for him," Karen said. Joe looked at her reproachfully.

"We went to McKinley Deaver's two mitigation banks, too," Emily said.

"Really?" Now Karen set her fork down. "What were they like?"

"The one up in Milton is all uplands. Deaver says it's just because he hasn't gotten around to mitigating yet."

"You talked to him?"

"Yup. The one over in Lake County is freshwater wetlands, but only because that's how nature made it. He hasn't done a thing to that land."

"Meaning any developer who buys into that mitigation bank is going to eliminate wetlands that aren't recouped elsewhere, in direct violation of the Clean Water Act." Karen's eyes got a little flashy as she said this. It was a good look for her, I thought.

"Exactly. You know Belie had visited the bank in Milton, right?"

"No!"

"Yup," Emily chimed in. "Gail found a scrap of paper from a printout he'd made of our meeting minutes, where you talked about the Eglin development and mitigation banks."

"That must be what made him decide to target you!" Joe said. Suddenly *his* eyes were flashy.

"Nothing to be done about that now," Karen said. She turned back to us. "There had to be something about the Eglin deal that set him off, don't you think?"

"That's how it feels to me," I said.

"Tomorrow morning I'm going to find my notes about the deal, go over everything again. There must be something I missed the first time. The comment period is closed but the Okaloosa Commission still hasn't voted on the issue."

"We still have time then," I said.

Joe looked like he was about to say something. His anger was maybe down a notch, more like exasperation now, but I could tell he wasn't pleased about the idea of his wife going down this path. But then he looked at her and saw how lively her face had become—so different than when we arrived an hour ago. I watched him make the decision to shut his piehole and let her fight her battle.

That there's a good husband, I thought.

"What about Australia?" I asked.

Karen and Joe both looked puzzled. "What about it?"

"Do they have mitigation banking down there or something?"

"Not that I know of. Why do you ask?"

"It keeps coming up," Emily explained. "Belie had a link labeled Australia on his blog, but there was no content behind it. And Gail overheard Deaver talking about Australia to someone on the phone, at the end of our visit."

"Belie had a blog?"

"Yeah. Not much to it, though," Em said, jotting down the web address for Karen.

"I'll look into that, too."

We left shortly after that, Karen promising to be in touch as soon as she'd done her research.

The next morning Mike stuck his head in my office at around 8:30. "Can I have a word?"

"Of course," I said, startled. I followed him into his office and shut the door. These closed-door meetings were starting to get on my nerves. But once again Mike surprised me, in a good way.

"I've been thinking about code enforcement. We're going to need another assistant for you, now that Shawn is out."

"Are you sure? With the economy down, and less building . . ."

"I know, things are slower," he said. "There are fewer new

building projects, so there's less dirt in the street. But I want you to take on more of the planning work, in terms of subdivision review. Patrick's been talking to Avalex again and it looks like they've finally decided to come in after all. Maybe." Avalex was a tech company that had been flirting with the idea of building its new headquarters in Gulf Breeze. "If it happens, I want you to take the lead on that project. I need to stay focused on the Master Plan for a while. And code enforcement isn't going away anytime soon. You know what Gulf Breeze residents are like anyway, and with so many empty homes in the new subdivisions, code enforcement complaints are only going to increase."

"Makes sense," I said, doing a little internal cheer about Avalex. It would be my first commercial project. "Do you want me to work on an ad?"

"I was thinking of offering the job to Emily."

"Cool!" This was shaping up to be an unexpectedly good day.

Mike smiled at my enthusiasm. "I figured since you two are inseparable anyway, we might as well make it official. Do you think she could do the work?"

"Oh yeah. She knows a lot of the development code already."

"What about the people aspect? Could she stand up to developers and builders without being bullied?"

"Sure," I said, thinking I would have to give Em a crash course in assertiveness training.

"Okay, great. I'll call her in and let her know as soon as we're done here."

"Will we be running an ad for a new admin, then?"

"Not right away. Building has slowed down so much I think Rosario can cover both phones. Emily may need to help her now and then if she gets overwhelmed. You might need to pitch in sometimes, too."

"Absolutely. But will she mind?"

"From Rosario's point of view, she's been covering the Planning & Zoning phones an awful lot lately anyway." He smiled to show it wasn't a criticism. "I think she'll appreciate the job security. She was hoping to cut back her hours starting next year, but Jim's business has really taken a hit from this economy." Rosario's husband Jim was a plumber. "I'll give her a little bump in pay and tell her she can stay on full time as long as she likes, and we'll hire a part-time assistant whenever she says the word. I think that will make her happy."

"Great. Do you need anything from me?"

"There is one more thing I need you to do. The Chief is holding Shawn over at the jail. There's a bail hearing set for later this afternoon. I need you to total up all the GulfBreeze-Singles signs you and he pulled and the number of hours you spent doing it. If I can make the case that he caused more than $5,000 in damage to city property, we can charge him with a felony."

I returned to my desk with a sigh. I'd never been asked to keep track of the number of signs we found. I poked around on my hard drive for a few minutes, looking for something that might help, but that was futile. Then I stood up and headed out of the office. There was nothing for it but to count the signs heaped up in the pile next to the utility shed.

I waved at Rosario as I passed through the reception area. Emily wasn't at her desk. Maybe Mike was already speaking to her about the new position.

Outside I stared at the sign pile with resignation. It was taller than me. I spent a few minutes attempting to estimate the number of signs through some sort of geometric triangulation, but that was a bust, too. Finally, I began lifting the signs off the pile and heaving them behind me, creating a new pile. I counted out loud as I went, so I wouldn't lose track.

Just as I got to, "23! 24!" a voice behind me said, "You

sound like a drill sergeant counting jumping jacks."

"Oh no no no, I'm going to lose count!"

"Twenty four," Emily said, coming around beside me and looking at the two piles, the growing one and the shrinking one. "I've got your back."

"I know you do, and now it's official." I grinned at her.

"Yeah." She looked kind of worried.

"What's wrong? This is going to be great!"

"I guess. I'm excited, I'm just nervous, too. I'll feel better when I'm certified. Mike's going to have me start the Level I code enforcement certification course immediately."

"When will you be sworn in?"

"Mike wants to wait until I have my certification."

"Well, shoot. How long will that take?" I'd thought he intended the change right away. I felt my enthusiasm start to wane as my dream of doing real planning work receded into the distant future.

Em sensed my disappointment. "I should be done by next week," she said quickly. "It's a 40-hour online course. Mike said I could spend some time in the office working on it, and I'll do the rest in the evening at home. Then I just have to go to Tallahassee to take the exam. They offer it every Saturday. I'm going to try to go this week. And by the way, 24."

"But that only gives you two days to prepare."

"Don't worry, I can do it."

"That sounds great. I'd take you to lunch to celebrate, but I have to get these sign numbers to Mike before Shawn's bail hearing."

"Can I help?"

"Why not? You can start by piling these signs over there while I count off. Ready? Twenty-five, twenty-six . . ."

The final count was 543 signs. I decided to round up to 600. I'd discarded some of the signs early on, before Mike decided he wanted them all saved. Besides, I'd been serious when I said it was likely Shawn had taken signs off the pile and placed them back out in the field. Since we had to remove those signs twice, it was only fair to count them twice.

But even with a total of 600, I could only come up with $2,250 in costs. That was working under the assumption that Shawn and I had spent an average of 15 minutes per sign for removal. What else was there?

Then I remembered the time I'd spent researching the dating site's ISP and creating a dating profile. Even better, there was the time Mike spent composing the cease-and-desist letter and adding the webpage that asked the Breezers for their help. That page had taken Mike the better part of a workday, and for those hours I got to bill at Mike's average hourly rate, which was much higher than mine.

Finally, I arrived at a figure just over $5,000. I worked up a form breaking out the hours into several categories. When I was finished I emailed it to Mike.

A minute later he was standing in my office. "This looks like an invoice. Are we billing Shawn for his services?"

"I thought that's what you wanted. If not, just tell me what format to use."

"No, this is good." He turned and exited.

I felt grumpy. I didn't like it when Mike was less than ecstatic about my work.

I decided the solution was food. I looked at the clock. It was just before noon. Rosario should be back from lunch any minute.

I grabbed my purse and went to fetch Emily for Thai food.

When we got back to the office, David was sitting in the reception area chatting with Rosario.

"You know what I've been wondering?" Rosario said as Emily settled into her workstation and I joined David at the table where he sat. "Whatever happened to the developer?"

"Huh?" David asked.

"The guy who parachuted out of the plane and took off. After bailing on those poor folks in Yellow Tree. He was the reason y'all drove up to Milton in the first place, wasn't he? When you found Karen Baretta?" She looked at me for confirmation. I nodded.

"Dan Bradford," David said. "They haven't found him yet. Looks like he successfully pulled a D.B. Cooper."

"A who?"

"You haven't heard of D.B. Cooper?" We all shook our heads no. "I guess it's because you've never lived out West."

Though he was originally from Tybee Island, Georgia, David had lived in Utah for 22 years before taking the City Engineer job in Gulf Breeze. He'd decided to come back to the South so his kids would experience it growing up.

"In 1971, D.B. Cooper hijacked a Northwest Airlines jet flying from Portland to Seattle. He said he was carrying a bomb and demanded $200,000 in unmarked 20s and four parachutes. The plane landed in Seattle and the money was delivered. Cooper let the passengers go but kept four members of the crew onboard. He told them to head to Reno. Somewhere over southwest Washington State, he jumped out of the plane and was never seen again."

We all continued to stare at him blankly.

"I can't believe you've never heard of him. Up in the Northwest, he's a folk hero. There are bars named after him and stuff. Not that I ever go to such places," he added.

David had converted to Mormonism while he lived in Utah. According to his own accounts, this had saved him from the alcoholism that was rampant in his family. He sounded alternatively relieved to have been spared the family addiction and wistful about it. "The legend of D.B. Cooper made its way down here eventually, too. There's a woman up in Pace who says her husband, who died in '95, was really Cooper, though she knew him as Duane Weber." Pace was up in north Santa Rosa.

"Does she have the money?" Emily asked.

"No one knows. The only portion of the money that was ever recovered was $5,000. Some 8-year-old kid found it on the banks of the Columbia River in 1980."

"That doesn't sound so good for old D.B.," I said.

"Yeah. The FBI claims he didn't survive the jump. Though on the other hand, every few years they start looking into a new candidate for who the real D.B. might be. Personally I like to believe he walked out of the Cascades, hightailed it down to Mexico—that's where he originally wanted the flight crew to take him—and has been living the good life on some Mexican beach ever since."

David struggled a little with domestic life sometimes. Fantasies of rich, single men living alone on tropical beaches—presumably drinking beer to their heart's content—helped get him through the day.

Just then Mike walked into the office wearing a scowl.

"What's up?" I asked, concerned. He'd been so happy since Shawn had been apprehended and the GulfBreezeSingles nightmare appeared to be behind us.

He came over and leaned on the counter. "Shawn couldn't give us squat."

"What do you mean?" Emily asked. "Is he trying to claim he didn't place the signs? We caught him red-handed!"

"But a lawyer might have told him to change his story for a not-guilty plea," I suggested.

"No, no," Mike said. "He admits he placed the signs. But he can't give us the company behind it."

David said, "I find it hard to believe he'd show them any

loyalty. Guy's a rat."

"More like the three blind mice. Idiot had no idea who he was working for. He got the job by replying to a Craigslist ad. 'Make money from home,' that kind of thing. When he replied he received an email with instructions."

"How much were they paying him per sign?" David asked.

"He wouldn't tell us. He dodged, said he didn't remember off the top of his head and would have to look at his bank statements. Of course, The Chief could look at the statements if he wanted to. He just hasn't gotten around to it yet. I think Shawn didn't want us to know what a pittance they were paying him."

"Can't they trace the emails?" Emily asked.

"They tried. Turns out they're originating from the same proxy server that's hosting the dating site itself. Didn't you guys say the kidnapper had his site on there, too?"

"Yes," Emily said. "I'm beginning to think that ISP is the source of all evil in Gulf Breeze."

I spent the rest of the week getting ready for the job transition. I cleaned out all my old code enforcement files and paperwork so I could hand things over to Emily in good order. Em, meanwhile, was occupied with her online class. Several times on Friday she came into my office with a procedure question, or wanting to know how something she'd heard about in the class pertained specifically to Gulf Breeze.

On Saturday afternoon, I was sitting in the bleachers at Chris's Young Adult League basketball game when my cell rang. It was Emily, ecstatically reporting that she'd passed the Code Enforcement I exam. After we hung up I called Mike. I wanted to make sure he didn't waste any time with the arrangements. He said he'd get in touch with The Chief and arrange to swear in Emily on Monday.

I knew it would only make her anxious, so I didn't tell Em

about the hijinks The Chief had in store. Therefore it was a complete surprise to her on Monday morning when, with Mike, David, Rosario, Patrick, and me present as witnesses, plus Terry the city recorder taping the event, The Chief showed up at the office, had her lay her hand on the Bible, and asked her to repeat the following:

I do solemnly swear that I will support the Constitution of the United States and the Ordinances and Codes of the City of Gulf Breeze, and that I will faithfully execute, to the best of my ability, the office of Code Enforcement Officer according to law; and I do further solemnly swear that since the adoption of the present Municipal Code I have not fought a duel with deadly weapons within this City nor out of it, nor have I sent or accepted a challenge to fight a duel with deadly weapons, nor have I acted as second in carrying a challenge, nor aided or assisted any person thus offending, so help me God.

Em managed to repeat the Oath without stumbling. But after The Chief, Patrick, and Terry offered their congratulations and departed, she turned to the rest of us.

"John Greenleaf *Whittier,* what the hell was that?"

Only then did we crack up.

"Patrick told The Chief he could pick any oath he wanted for swearing in city officers," I explained, once the hilarity had subsided. "And that's the one he chose. It's from the Commonwealth of Kentucky, slightly modified to suit our purposes."

"It's a good thing you hadn't encountered Belie before you were sworn in," Emily observed.

CHAPTER TWENTY-FOUR

Land schemes in Florida have a long and infamous history. Setting aside Ponce de Leon and the Fountain of Youth debacle, we could say that history began during the Jazz Age, with the Florida Land Boom of the 1920s. At the height of the madness, Miami properties could change hands up to 10 times a day at auction. Brokers and dealers speculated wildly in commodities as well as on the land, ordering building supplies vastly in excess of what was needed. Freight cars were loaded up with lumber and sent south with bills of lading no more specific than "Tampa" or "Boca Raton."

By January 1925, the press began to realize Florida had a bubble on its hands. That month, *Forbes* warned that Florida land prices had been completely severed from actual value. Its attention aroused, the IRS began to investigate. In October, tired of the builders' shenanigans, Florida's three major railroads placed an embargo on the state, refusing to deliver anything but food, fuel, and essential commodities. Then, three months later, the *Prinz Valdemar,* an old Danish warship that had been slated for conversion to a floating hotel, sank upon its arrival, blocking the entrance to Miami harbor.

With both shipping and rail blocked, the influx of resources slowed to a trickle and a more realistic picture of the market began to emerge. The game was pretty much up by 1926. Although by spring the harbor was cleared and the railroads had lifted their embargo, the flow of money had dried up by then.

The icing on the cake of disillusion came on September 14, 1926, when a Category 4 hurricane made landfall just south of Miami. The storm cut northwest across the state, entered the Gulf, then made landfall again at Pensacola/Mobile as a Category 3 storm. Along the way, it destroyed more than 13,000 homes, many in the Miami area, and created a tidal wave in Lake Okeechobee that drowned hundreds of people.

But by the 1950s, the lessons of the '20s had been forgotten, and the madness started again, so much so that the period from the mid-'50s until the early '70s is known as "Florida's Golden Age of Land Scams." By 1963, the scams had grown so rampant that New York and California enacted legislation to restrict false advertising in land sales. Florida responded later that year by passing the Florida Installment Land Sales Act, which was intended to regulate land subdivision and restore the state's tarnished reputation. In 1968, the Federal government waded in with the Interstate Land Sales Full Disclosure Act, which enabled HUD to oversee large subdivisions and required developers to provide a property report to all prospective buyers.

Karen Baretta knew this development history of her adopted state as well as she knew her own biography. And, despite the legislation of the '60s, she knew the ways in which land games in Florida had continued right up to the present. In the 1970s, it had been condos; then in the '80s, the timeshare epidemic began. More recently, scammers had used the Internet to circumvent domestic regulations and bring the "I have some swampland in Florida for you" scheme to international buyers who weren't yet aware of the cliché.

Still, she thought the mitigation banks might be the best con yet. After all, the previous schemes had tapped into a selfish goal only: to live in paradise. The mitigation banks offered the addition of piety: to save the planet. And yet, at heart, they were exactly the same.

Karen spent the weekend learning as much as she could about as many mitigation banks around the state as possible. What she found was that Belie, on that little watershed blog he'd set up, had indeed been right: many Florida Politicians, Planners, and Business Men were indeed involved in the mitigation industry. In fact, most of the banks she'd researched were owned by former planners (Gail would be appalled, she thought with a smile) or current politicians. And yes, by Democrats and Republicans alike—Belie was right about that as well.

It wasn't hard to see how the planners wound up in the mitigation game, in Karen's estimation. Let's say you're a city planner in a small Florida community. A project involving development of wetlands crosses your desk. Rather than attempting to mitigate wetlands loss directly, the developer has decided to use a mitigation bank to handle the EPA's wetlands mitigation requirement.

You've never seen the mitigation model firsthand, so you start asking questions, of the developer on the wetlands project, and even, if you can get access to him, of the manager of the bank. From their answers, you notice that . . . well, let's say you notice that a mitigation bank can be run without a lot of overhead.

At some point, you decide to go onsite and have a look at the mitigation bank for yourself. When you get there, you might find wetlands, uplands, or some combination thereof. If what you see is mostly uplands, or if you see wetlands but you can tell the land was wetlands already, meaning no actual reclamation is occurring, you might try to broach the subject with the mitigation bank owner.

"I don't mean to stir up trouble. I can see all this EPA

paperwork is in order, but I don't want us to run into a problem with the new development later, and for the Feds to come down here and say we weren't doing our job. And I couldn't help noticing that you haven't actually produced any new wetlands to make up for the wetlands that will be lost when Frank builds that high school. I just want to make sure we're all covered: the city, Frank, and you."

The mitigation bank owner laughs. "Not to worry," he says. "You see, federal guidelines allow wetlands developers to purchase credits for uplands, as long as they occur within a mitigation bank. Here in Florida more than a third of the mitigation credits that have been approved so far have been for dry land."

"But that means a net loss of wetlands," you protest. "I thought the goal was no net loss."

The bank owner laughs again. "Who are we to question the Feds?"

And finally it dawns on you: the mitigation bank is receiving more than twice the going market price per acre to put a fence around some undeveloped land and plant a sign at the entrance. That's it.

And if your mind is of a certain entrepreneurial bent, it's not too long before you're thinking about opening a mitigation bank yourself.

CHAPTER TWENTY-FIVE

A couple hours after Em's swearing-in, she popped her head in my door. "I just had a message from Karen. She says she has some news for us and wonders if we can come for dinner."

We looked at each other guiltily. I'd hardly thought of Karen during the past week, and I suspected it was the same for Emily.

"We should go, huh."

"I think so."

Dinner was vegan pizza. When we were finished, Joe poured us each another glass of wine, and then we ladies moved to the living room while Joe stayed in the kitchen to clean up, insisting he didn't want any help. I think he'd decided our visits were therapeutic for Karen.

Emily and I settled on the couch. Karen sat opposite us in an easy chair under a floor lamp. She had a sheaf of papers, which she spread out on the coffee table in front of her after perching a pair of reading glasses on her nose.

Karen shuffled her papers for a moment, then looked up. "I've done some digging. I thought I'd start by finding out as much as I could about mitigation banks, especially in Florida.

"There are approximately 400 mitigation banks throughout the country, 40 of them in Florida. That may not seem like a huge percentage, but Florida is very important because the EPA is talking about making the Florida mitigation model the template for the whole country. I've looked at the ownership records for the 40 banks, but I can't find a unifying principle. The owners include former developers and former city planners, prominent Democrats and prominent Republicans. They cross every aisle you can think of."

"Then the unifying principle is money," I said.

Karen nodded.

"I have some information about that," Emily piped up. "I was interested in the financials for the industry and the profit margins, so I did some research. The going price for a mitigation bank credit here on the panhandle is $17,000/credit. Right now in Milton, land is going for about $8,000 an acre. So just by calling a parcel a mitigation bank, you've more than doubled your money."

"And the stakes will be even higher in south Florida, where land can go for 10 times what it does up here," Karen observed. She addressed me. "You can see why so many former planners have decided to get into the business."

In fact, I found it unnerving. "It's like hearing that Superman and Wonder Woman are going into business with Lex Luther. But I wonder what aspect of the industry set off Belie?"

"He only went crazy enough to kidnap Karen after he read about her on the PFC site," Emily said. "It must have something to do with that."

"You said your group focused on how the base did a runaround past the requirement to offer the acreage to the Park Service, right?"

"Yup."

"Well, something about that had to be the trigger."

"Maybe because he'd been in the military, he didn't like the idea of wetlands at Eglin being developed?" Emily suggested.

"Maybe," Karen said dubiously. "Though I don't think he had any particular connection to Eglin."

"He didn't tell you anything about it? During those four days?"

Karen shook her head. "No. He told me what he wanted me to do, and I got started. I should have asked him more questions, but I didn't."

We all sighed. Then I suggested, "Why don't y'all tell me again about the Eglin deal and what PFC had to say about it. Especially the public stuff, since that's what caught Belie's eye."

Karen nodded. "The Eglin Air Force base is making a 19-acre parcel of land available for commercial development. This isn't the first time the Air Force has leased land on the base out to private interests. The base is huge—700 square miles—and I guess they feel like they have room to spare. In fact, the parcel in question is an island of undeveloped land surrounded by other parcels that have already been leased out and made available to commercial developers.

"When the base has leased land in the past, it's almost always wetlands. Much of the base is wetlands anyway, and the land that commercial developers covet is going to be waterfront. PFC objected because the National Park Service is supposed to have first dibs on any parcels the base decides to unload. But the base skipped that step this time."

"Do you think they bypassed the Park Service because the parcel is relatively small and surrounded by commercial development already?"

"Probably. But our concern is precedent. If you're thinking the Seashore probably would have taken a pass on this parcel anyway, since it's already boxed in by commercial development and therefore of limited environmental use, then I agree. But what I worry about is that now they've established precedent for not contacting the Seashore first. What is the next parcel going to look like, where they don't do what they're supposed to?"

"What did the Park Service say?"

Karen and Em both looked at me blankly.

The next day Emily and I paid a visit to the National Seashore Visitors' Center on our lunch break.

"I still think maybe we should have tried to make an appointment," Em said on the drive over.

"I favor the pop in. Less chance for people to feed you a prepackaged response. But if he's not available, we'll ask for an appointment."

"Who are we looking for?"

"Tim Davidson. He's the Acting Superintendent of the National Seashore since the Director stepped down last November."

The parking lot of the Visitors' Center was mostly empty and there were no visitors in sight when we entered the building, just a park ranger sitting behind the information counter. He had long blond hair in a ponytail.

"Can I help you?"

"We're here to see Mr. Davidson."

"Do you have an appointment?"

"No."

Blond ponytail headed down the hall, returning a moment later. "He can see you if it's quick. He has a meeting over in Navarre at one o'clock."

"We'll only be a minute," I assured him.

"Who did you say you were again?"

"I'm Gail LaRue from Gulf Breeze Planning & Zoning. And this is Emily Wright, our code enforcement officer."

"Tim usually meets with Patrick from the city."

"Well, today he's getting us."

"Lucky him."

Blond ponytail led us out of the public area and down a hall past several office doors. All were closed until the last one. He stuck his head in. "This is Gail and Emily from Gulf Breeze Planning & Zoning."

Tim Davidson was a slim man, probably late 30s, with long-ish brown hair and glasses in a frame that had to be at least 10 years old. He stood up and leaned over his desk to shake our hands.

"What can I do for you?" he asked once we were all seated. "Can I get you anything?"

"We're good, thanks," I said. "We're here because we have some questions for you about the Eglin development."

Davidson looked at us blankly. "What?"

"The 19-acre parcel that Eglin is getting ready to lease out for commercial development."

"Rings a vague bell. What about it?"

"Eglin's agreement with the Park Service specifies that any land the base intends to offer for commercial development is supposed to be offered to the Park Service first, to extend the Gulf Islands National Seashore," Emily said. "But that step was skipped for the current project."

"Was it?"

"It was."

"Well, I don't know about that. There's a commissioner over at Eglin who oversees such things. He probably determined the parcel wasn't suitable for park land."

"But shouldn't you be determining that?" Emily said. "You're acting director of this park, right? If it was left up to Eglin to decide whether land should be transferred to the national park system, or leased for a profit, I kind of have a feeling the answer might be 'leased for profit' every time, don't you?"

"That's not it," Davidson began and then stopped abruptly.

"So you do know about the parcel?"

"Well, not all the details, but I know it's not an issue, from the Park Service's point of view."

"If you don't know the details, how can you be sure of that?" Emily's voice rose an octave.

"Look, I appreciate your concern, but I assure you, there's nothing to worry about." Davidson didn't look it, though. He actually looked quite worried. I thought our presence in his office, asking him these questions, was ruining his day.

I went to his rescue. "I suppose the fact that the parcel is surrounded on three sides by commercial development makes it less appealing for the Park Service."

Davidson's face lit up. "Yes, exactly. It's hard for the park service to manage small parcels flanked by commercial projects. The traffic, the noise pollution . . . it becomes a law of diminishing returns."

"Makes sense. Well, we won't take up any more of your time. Thanks for meeting with us." I rose and offered my hand. Davidson looked ready to kiss it, he was so happy I'd let him off the hook.

"What was that all about?" Emily demanded once we were back in the truck.

"We learned all we're going to from Mr. Davidson."

"All I learned is that he's a sneaking little liar."

"Exactly."

Emily pressed her lips together for a moment. "I'm sorry, but that doesn't really help me."

"We know he's scared. We know he's lying. We know he isn't a decision maker in this little turn of events. Someone told him the Park Service was going to be out of the Eglin deal, and someone told him to keep his mouth shut. That's probably all he really knows."

"That's not all he knows. He knows who told him to keep his mouth shut."

She had a point. "Touché."

★ ★ ★ ★ ★

For once there were no messages waiting for me back at the office. I settled at my desk, brought the Panhandlers for Change website up, and navigated through the meeting minutes, looking for something we might have overlooked.

The parcel was to be developed by Chip Brown. Who was Chip Brown?

I dialed Em's extension.

"Yes'm?"

"What do we know about Chip Brown?"

"Who?"

"He's the developer who's supposed to be working on the Eglin project."

"Ah. Good call. But I don't know anything about him."

"Let's see what we can find out."

An hour later I hadn't come up with anything in the city files, but a quick Internet search taught me that Mr. Brown specialized in small to midsized commercial projects on Okaloosa Island. I'd also found an address and phone number for an office located in Mary Esther. I called, got voice mail, and left a message.

At five o'clock, Emily flopped into the office. "Whatdja find?"

"He has an office in Mary Esther. I tried the number."

"Any luck?"

"Left a message."

"So what's our next move?"

"We're going to the review meeting for the Eglin project."

"I thought approval had already been granted?"

"Nope. When Karen submitted her letter that was for an open comment period Okaloosa County holds *before* the commission discusses any proposed development on Eglin land. The commissioners take a couple of weeks to review the comments and to have county staff follow up if necessary. *Then* they put it up for a vote."

"When?"

"Tomorrow night."

At 6:45 the following evening, we pulled into the parking lot of the Okaloosa County office complex in Karen and Joe's Toyota Prius, with Joe behind the wheel. They'd decided to join us at the meeting. I was glad. I thought Karen was probably our best weapon.

The parking lot was mostly empty. "Looks like the community isn't too worried about Eglin selling off wetlands," Emily observed as we all climbed out of the car.

"I'm telling you, it's been a complete non-event. Even the environmental community hasn't paid a lot of attention to this one," Karen said. She sounded frustrated.

We climbed the stairs into the County building. Karen and Joe, having attended Okaloosa County Commission meetings before, led the way down a cool tiled hall to the meeting room.

An older woman with a modified beehive hairdo and cat's-eye glasses sat near the entrance, behind a small table with a pile of agendas and a sign-in sheet. We signed in and took our agendas to the front row. The few other attendees were scattered around the room.

There were four items on the agenda. The first was preliminary review of a 20-lot residential subdivision in unincorporated Fort Walton, and the second was a rezone request for a parcel on the outskirts of Destin. The third and fourth items concerned the Eglin matter. The third item was a rezoning request changing the parcel from I-1, which was evidently Okaloosa County's military usage zoning designation, to C-1, which was commercial. It hadn't occurred to me that a rezone would be necessary before the project moved forward, but it made sense.

The final agenda item was "Preliminary Approval for a Conditional Use Permit requested by Eglin Air Force Base and Developer Chip Brown, Involving the Transfer by Lease of 19 Acres of Eglin Land for the Purpose of Commercial Development."

There were several attachments included with the agenda. Paging through them, I saw that the public comments had been included. Besides Karen's eloquent note, there were six other comments. Five were in favor of the development, citing the usual reasons: construction is good for the economy, new development will add to the area's appeal as a tourist mecca, etc. There was one other comment besides Karen's that questioned the wisdom of the land transfer. It was more virulent than Karen's measured tones.

"I urge the Commission to reject this proposal and retain the 19 acres from Eglin as part of the Air Force Base or as part of the Gulf Islands National Seashore as intended by Congressman Bob Sikes. The loss of wetlands in our state has already led to coastal watershed flooding resulting in millions of dollars in damage, not to mention lost lives. We are already losing many acres of wetlands every year to the fraudulently named mitagation banks, which in point of fact don't actually mitagate anything. Don't let Eglin contribute to this travesty!"

"Look at this," I said.

Karen peered over my left shoulder. "Belie strikes again."

Emily peeked over my right. "He just couldn't stop himself from putting that 'a' in there, could he? If he ever comes out of that coma, I'm going to show him how to use spell check myself. Look what the cat dragged in," she added.

We turned toward the door. Tim Davidson and McKinley Deaver had just walked in. Together. Davidson avoided our stares as he found a seat toward the back of the room. Deaver, however, smiled broadly.

"Evenin', Ladies."

"Who's that?" Joe asked. I explained.

"I don't know Davidson," Karen said. "He's new. The old director retired a few months ago. They haven't found a permanent replacement yet."

The Chair banged his gavel, calling the meeting to order.

I daydreamed through the first two agenda items. I couldn't help it; it was too much like being at work. Finally they reached item 3. The County's senior planner, Phil Miller, whom I'd heard of but not met, made a boilerplate presentation.

Emily leaned over and whispered, "Is there any sense in us challenging the rezoning request?"

"I've been racking my brains to think of a reason, but I'm coming up empty."

"Now I know why we always put rezoning requests on the agenda *before* development requests."

The Chair asked if there were any comments from the public. I popped out of my chair.

"Yes, Miss . . . ?" the Chair said, smiling at me.

"LaRue," I said, returning the smile. "I'm wondering about the wisdom of changing the zoning on the parcel before the project is approved."

"While I understand your concern, Miss LaRue, one of the tricky aspects of Planning & Zoning is that we can't consider a use for a piece of property unless it's a permitted use, according to the zoning."

"I understand that," I said pleasantly. "I'm a planner myself. But my concern has to do with precedent. If the commission finds reason not to approve the proposed development, but the zoning is changed, then it's that much easier for another

203

developer to come in later and propose a commercial development."

"That's the idea of the rezoning, Miss LaRue."

"And I'm wondering if it's a *good* idea. We're talking about wetlands that has had the benefit of federal oversight for the past 50 years because of its inclusion on a military base. Surely the predisposition should be *against* development unless there's a pressing community need that can only be met by development."

One of the other commissioners spoke up. "I think the young lady raises an excellent point." His nameplate indicated he was Commissioner Williams. He had a big round head and round glasses. I bestowed a smile on him and sat back down. I hadn't really expected much of a discussion over the rezone. But now we knew which of the five Commissioners might be an ally.

The Commission voted unanimously to approve the rezone.

"Our next item of business," the Chair said, "is a request for preliminary approval of a conditional use permit allowing the rezoned 19 acres of Eglin property to be used for a commercial resort. Is the applicant present?"

There was silence after this question. The Chair looked up, surprised. "Mr. Brown isn't here? Or Mr. Swanson, or someone else from the base?"

"Mr. Brown wasn't able to make it tonight; he's indisposed," McKinley Deaver said. "But I may be able to answer some questions about his intention with the development. I don't know why the base didn't send anyone out."

The Chair turned to his right and exchanged a glance with the commissioner sitting there, whose nameplate identified him as Commissioner Tucker. "Well, let's proceed," the Chair said finally, looking disgruntled. "Mr. Miller, can you summarize this item for us?"

When Miller had finished his brief summary the Chair asked

if the commissioners had any questions.

"Was the public properly notified about the hearing for this conditional use permit application?" Commissioner Williams asked. "And were the property owners of the surrounding parcels informed?"

"They were, and I believe some of them are here tonight," Miller said. There followed a small parade of property owners stepping up to endorse the plan wholeheartedly. During the course of this love fest it was revealed that the proposed resort was intended to cater to military personnel stationed at the nearby bases. It would offer discount rates for spouses and children coming to visit enlisted men and women, or for out-of-town family members coming to witness a relative's graduation from basic or advanced training.

I thought this sounded like a pretty good idea, and I felt the tide of my indignation about the Eglin project recede a few inches.

When the enthusiastic neighbors had run out of breath, the Chair thanked them for their input. Then Commissioner Williams spoke up.

"Before we go on, John, I'd like to address some of the responses we received during the public comment period. It appears to me that the points covered in the positive comments we received have already been discussed here—in fact, some of the people we just heard from may have written those comments. But I'm interested in this one." He proceeded to read Belie's rant aloud.

McKinley Deaver stood up. "Mr. Commissioner, if I may, you should be aware the authorities believe that comment was submitted by Belie Jenkins of Milton, who is now lying in Gulf Breeze Hospital in a coma after kidnapping a lady and forcing her to write letters to the editor against mitigation banking."

"I heard about that," Commissioner Williams said, looking troubled.

Karen rose to her feet. "I'm the lady who was kidnapped and forced to write letters."

"Are you now?" Commissioner Williams looked at her with interest.

"I am, and though of course I feel that Mr. Jenkins's methods were seriously misguided, I share his concerns about wetlands development, mitigating banking, and this development in particular."

"I hope you're not suffering from Stockholm syndrome, Ms. Baretta." The Chair had a gleam in his eye as he said this, almost as though he knew the suggestion would drive Karen batty. But she took a deep breath and kept her cool.

"My position on such matters is well documented and predates the incident with Mr. Jenkins by at least 15 years. However, in the case of this proposed development for Eglin, my main concern is the way the Park Service has been left out of the loop. It's my understanding that any time Eglin decides it has land to spare, that land is supposed to be offered to the National Parks as a possible extension of the Gulf Islands National Seashore. I saw no evidence anywhere in the presentation that this step had been taken."

"Mr. Chair, Tim Davidson, Acting Superintendent, Gulf Islands National Seashore," squeaked a voice from the back. We all turned to look at Davidson, who appeared to shrink under our collective gaze. He looked like he would rather be gutting a catfish than standing before the County Commission. Nonetheless, he continued. I could almost picture the imaginary weapon Deaver had pressed to the small of his back.

"I'm here to say the Park Service has no interest in this Eglin parcel. Because of its small size and the fact that it's already surrounded by commercial development, we don't feel it would make a good addition to the National Seashore."

"Thank you, Mr. Davidson," the Chair said, beaming.

"If I may, Mr. Chairman." Karen spoke up again. "With no disrespect to Mr. Davidson, I'm not sure the Acting Superintendent is supposed to make this decision alone. But I'm less concerned with the decision and more concerned with the precedent it would set to skip the formal Park Service review that has always been part of releasing land from the base. Next time the parcel might not be 19 acres nestled between a hotel and a restaurant. Next time it might be 100 acres of turtle nesting ground."

"Are you suggesting Eglin is trying to give the Park Service the runaround?" Commission Tucker looked fiery.

"I'm suggesting that conservation isn't the niche of Eglin's land-use team. Its concern is the best interests of the base. Which may, of course, include financial and/or administrative interests. That's why the process of transferring lands from federal use to private use involves several different governing bodies, including this one, during the review process."

"As well as the public," Commissioner Williams said, beaming down at Karen. "I think Ms. Baretta raises some excellent points."

The Chair looked like he was sorry Belie hadn't finished the job. He turned toward Commissioner Williams. "A lot of people have worked on this project for a very long time, Bob. I don't know if I feel comfortable telling them they have to wait longer when the Director of the National Seashore came here in person to tell us Parks isn't interested in this parcel."

Commissioner Layton, who sat on the far side of Commissioner Williams and hadn't said a peep all evening, now spoke up. "Acting Superintendent, not Director. Anyway, I don't see how there could be any harm in contacting the Park Service and asking for something formal in writing before we move forward. Just to make sure all our *i*'s are dotted and our *t*'s are crossed. If, as Mr. Davidson says, the parks have no interest in the parcel, he should be able to get an answer back to us on their behalf quickly, or write it himself. But at least then we'd have an official record of it. For the future, as Ms. Baretta says."

"We'll put it to the vote. The agenda calls for a vote on preliminary approval of the project. Can I get a motion?"

Commissioner Tucker spoke up. "I move to grant preliminary approval of the Chip Brown development project to create a resort for military families."

"Second?" the Chair asked. No one seconded. His head appeared to swell to twice its normal size. "With no second the motion dies," he said finally.

"I'd like to make a counter motion," Commissioner Williams said. "I move to postpone the vote on preliminary approval for this project while our staff contacts the Park Service to ask for a formal, written response on whether or not they're interested in having the parcel become part of the National Seashore."

"Second," Commissioner Layton said promptly.

"All in favor?"

Commissioners Williams, Layton, and Black raised their hands.

"Opposed?"

Commissioner Tucker and the Chair were opposed. The motion passed.

I knew we shouldn't show any signs of gloating—that would be like waving a red flag in the faces of the Good Ole Boys. Obviously the others had the same idea. Karen and Joe, who were more experienced with this kind of thing than Em or I, sat looking modestly down at their own laps. Em's eyes were lowered, too, but suddenly she reached over and grabbed my hand. She squeezed so hard I lost circulation in my thumb before she let go.

Chapter Twenty-Six

Karen couldn't sleep. Joe had tumbled into bed half an hour after they got home from the meeting, but Karen was too restless. The elation of Gail and Emily on the drive home had been charming, but Karen couldn't share their feeling. She knew their victory with the County Commission had been a shallow one. There was little doubt the Commission would approve the Chip Brown development once it got a written response from the Park Service on the books.

Even more than that, though, she was frustrated by the sense that she was missing the big picture. What had Belie seen that she hadn't?

Though she'd gone over it a dozen times already, she pulled up the PFC site and read the meeting minutes that Belie had printed. Once again, nothing new jumped out at her.

Then she brought up Belie's own site, WatershedBlog.com. If only Belie had invested some time in adding more content to the site, she might have a clue what the hell he'd been thinking.

She looked at the row of dead links across the top of the page: Watersheds, Wetlands, Mitagation Banks, Australia, Links, Contact Us.

Australia. What was up with Australia?

She'd tried searching on mitigation banking in Australia previously, prompted by Emily and Gail. After about three dozen keyword combinations, she was confident there was no story there. But then why had Belie included it on his website?

Set aside the mitigation banks for a moment, she told herself. What other keywords summed up the Eglin development?

When she hit on the combination Australia + national parks + private development, she got something. The year before, the Australian Parliament had passed a law allowing the government to award concession and lodging franchises on land within its national park system to private developers.

This was even worse than the military parceling off portions of unused land. It was the equivalent of inviting the biggest of commercial interests to set up shop in the Grand Canyon.

Belie must have been horrified by the idea, as was Karen herself. But she still felt like she was missing something.

What does this have to do with the Florida Panhandle, Belie?

She kept digging.

CHAPTER TWENTY-SEVEN

When I arrived at the office on Thursday morning, Rosario was alone in the reception area. As soon as she saw me, she started rolling her eyes and blinking wildly.

"What's the matter?" I asked, alarmed. "Do you have something in your eye?"

Just then I felt something jab into the base of my neck.

"Look who it is," a male voice drawled in my ear. "The star of the show. Straight back down the hall, now, and no funny business. You too, lady," he said to Rosario. She stood up and crossed behind Emily's empty desk, mouthing "I'm sorry" at me before she turned and started down the hall.

What fresh hell was this? I followed Rosario, with the drawler close behind me. I could feel the gun barrel bumping against my head as I walked. Should I try to disarm him? Could I stop short without winding up with a bullet in my brain? What if I ducked my head while reaching back to grab his balls? But that was no good, it would leave Rosario vulnerable.

The drawler seemed to guess my thoughts. "I've heard about you, Wonder Woman," he snarled. "Try anything and I'll blow your head off in a heartbeat."

"Understood." I tried to catch a glimpse of him in the reflection from Mike's door as we passed, but I didn't dare turn my head too much. It felt like he had at least a few inches on me, but that was all I could tell.

At the end of the hall a closed door led to the back staircase.

211

"Up," the drawler said. Rosario opened the door and went through.

As we climbed the stairs, he wolf-whistled. "That's some ass you got on you, Wonder Woman. I'm going to have some fun with that before the day is done."

"Sounds great."

He grabbed me in a headlock. "You're a mouthy thing, aren't ya? I'll fill that mouth of yours. Maybe we'll just get started right now."

Ahead of us Rosario, who hadn't turned around, whimpered.

The drawler laughed. "Don't worry, Mama. You'll get your turn." He tightened his hold around my neck until I clawed his arm, desperate for air. Then he abruptly let go and gave me a shove. "Get goin'."

I felt an adrenaline surge. I took a couple of deep, measured breaths as we continued upstairs, willing my hands and legs to stop shaking. I had accomplished what I'd wanted. I'd seen him. He was big—over 6 feet, with a barrel chest and a big belly. Wearing a black t-shirt and a pair of pantyhose over his face. Evidently the dumbass didn't know the pantyhose-over-the-face thing is mainly for security cameras. Or fetish porn. In the close proximity of a headlock, I was able to see his features perfectly well. But it did me no good; I didn't know him.

I'd also seen the bottom half of a confederate flag tattoo on his bicep, where it peeked down below the sleeve of his shirt. This was worrisome. The fact that he was wearing the stupid pantyhose on his head suggested he wanted to remain unrecognizable, which was good if it meant he wasn't planning to kill us. But at some point it might occur to him that he'd let us see a large distinguishing mark, the tattoo. Then his plans might change.

Rosario reached the door at the top of the stairs and paused.

"Go on," the drawler said. She opened the door and went

through, holding it open behind her. I touched her fingertips briefly as I reached for the door, trying to put some reassurance in the gesture. Poor Rosario. It was my fault she was in this mess. If my suspicions were right, I'd baited the men who'd put together the Eglin deal by trying to draw them out. The County Commission meeting must have been the last straw. Now here they were. Or here were their goons, anyway. I'd stirred up some Good Ole Boy money pot. And now I had to face the swarm of angry bees. But how unfair that Rosario had to face it with me.

Again I wondered if it was time to act. I thought I could use the door to try to disarm the drawler. But again he seemed to anticipate me. Before I'd crossed the threshold I felt the gun barrel jabbed into the base of my skull again. *Fine. Not yet.*

The door opened onto a short corridor that led to the meeting room. Rosario went far enough into the room to allow me and the drawler to enter behind her. Then she stopped, uncertain what he wanted us to do next. She stepped over to the right, and I saw we weren't alone. Mike and David were sitting against the far wall with their hands on their heads, and Emily stood on the raised platform at the front of the room where the commissioners normally sat. A man stood behind her holding a gun to her head.

"Hail, hail, the gang's all here," that man said jovially. He was smaller than the drawler. Not much bigger than Emily, actually, but wiry. He was wearing jeans, workboots, and a navy t-shirt. His gun was a ring of fire 9mm. And he too had a stupid pair of pantyhose on his head.

"When we get out of this I'm going to offer a webinar on home invasion Dos and Don'ts," I muttered.

"What's that, blondie?" 9mm asked.

"I was wondering what you want with us. I mean, city employees, you know? Who could be more harmless?"

"I think you know why we're here."

"I have no idea."

"Well then, I want you to strip down to your underwear." 9mm laughed at his own non sequitur.

"That's not appropriate," Mike said from his spot on the floor.

"I decide what's appropriate," 9mm said. "And I think it would be appropriate for you to strip down to your underdrawers, too. All of you."

Behind me, the drawler giggled. 9mm seemed completely relaxed, which didn't seem right. Painkillers, maybe? I was pretty sure both these gentlemen had a deep familiarity with the recreational use of pharmaceuticals.

"And if we refuse?" David asked.

9mm reached out and grabbed a handful of Emily's black hair, then yanked down. She grimaced in pain but didn't make a sound. *That's my girl.*

"No need for that," I said quickly. "We're on it." I started unbuttoning my blouse. It was white swiss dot, sort of dainty. When it was off I folded it and placed it on the lectern that was pushed against the back wall. Then I unzipped my skirt. I noted almost with surprise that I was wearing my yellow satin bra and panty set, the ones with white polka dots. I didn't remember selecting them this morning. I must have been feeling particularly optimistic while I got dressed. Shows what I knew.

Behind me I heard Rosario start to disrobe as well. Exchanging a weary look between them, Mike and David rose to their feet and did the same.

9mm twisted the gun barrel against Emily's temple. "Get going, Betty," he said. With shaking fingers, Em started to remove her clothes.

When everyone was finished, I took stock. Mike was a boxers man, but David had on tightie whities. Em was wearing white cotton panties, a padded white bra, and knee-high white cotton socks. She'd started to remove them, but 9mm had stopped her. "Leave those on," he said with a leer in his voice that was just plain rude.

With an effort, I restrained myself from turning around to check out Rosario's unmentionables.

"Okay, let's get this party started," 9mm said. He grabbed Emily by the arm and started dragging her toward the hallway to the stairs. "Little Miss Kneesocks and I are going to excuse ourselves for a bit. My esteemed colleague will entertain you folks until we return."

Mike and David both started forward at this. 9mm curled Emily into a headlock and jabbed the gun back into her temple as he whirled back around toward them. Meanwhile, the drawler stepped forward with his gun pointed at the men.

"Sit your asses back down!" 9mm snarled, his dapper manner gone. Mike and David slowly backed up to the wall and slid down to the floor. There was a curious mixture of rage and despair on their faces. I could see a vein throbbing in David's temple. The drawler and 9mm were both in front of me now, leaving Rosario and me unattended. But I couldn't see a play. If Rosario had been someone else, maybe we could have gone after the two idiots simultaneously. But I couldn't expect that of Rosario. I figured I could make it downstairs to the phones and dial 911, but if I did so there was a possibility the thugs would shoot the others and bail. I doubted they were experienced killers, but not because of any great aversion to the idea. So I stayed put.

When Mike and David were seated again, the drawler moved over closer to them, keeping the gun pointed at David. 9mm turned back toward Rosario and me, dragging Emily toward the corridor. "You two get over there with the others," he barked.

Rosario started toward the wall—black satin panties and bra, not bad—but I stayed put.

"Take me instead."

9mm stopped short in front of me. "What makes you think I'm not going to have both of you?"

"Understood. But I want first dibs. I'll make it worth your while." I smiled at him.

Would he fall for it?

He would. He let go of Emily. "Fine then," he said, his debonair act returning. "Come along."

"You said I could have the blonde!" the drawler whined. Evidently they had some kind of George and Lennie thing going.

"All in good time."

I turned and sashayed toward the hallway. I heard 9mm giggle behind me. Definitely pills. I'd seen his drugged-out eyes through the ridiculous pantyhose. Prescription pill abuse was rampant on the panhandle.

I started down the stairs, but he stopped me. "In here," he said, opening the door to a tiny supply closet.

"There's not much room in there." I'd been hoping to get him downstairs, where I'd have a lot of options.

"It'll do."

He held the door open and I entered past him. He slapped my ass as I walked by. I'd known it was coming but it still made me jump. 9mm laughed.

When I got far enough into the room I turned back toward him. The room was lined along two walls with high metal shelves covered in paper, pens, notebooks, and other office supplies. Along the back wall there was a little table holding a postage meter and a paper cutter.

9mm let the door shut and we were enveloped in darkness.

"Jesus, I can't see shit."

"The light switch is to the right of the door."

He fumbled for a moment and then an overhead fluorescent light blinked on. "Thanks."

"My pleasure." I arranged myself with one leg crossed in front of the other, using my arms to push The Girls forward a little.

9mm giggled again. I couldn't believe my luck. I would've had trouble with the big guy. I would have done my best, but he was just so damn big. 9mm was a whole 'nother story. I had a few inches on him in height. My arms were longer, my shoulders broader. Couldn't he see it?

Nope. He saw nothing but The Girls at this point. "Take your bra off," he said in a rather choked voice.

"You bet." This bra opened in the front, I was glad to note. I unhooked the clasp and slowly drew the cups back from my skin, until The Girls popped out.

I abruptly dropped my arms to my sides, so the bra slid to the floor. Then I reached back up and cupped The Girls. Trusting that 9mm wasn't the subtle type, I squeezed them together and bounced them up and down.

Some sort of gurgling sound escaped 9mm. I stole a glance and was pleased to see him looking slack-jawed. This was going to be just too damn easy. I smiled. "Don't you want to touch them?" I asked. "I want you to."

I bounced them up and down again. "Damn straight," he breathed and stepped toward me.

When I emerged from the supply closet a few minutes later, I heard a ruckus coming from the main conference room. I moved quickly to the doorway and peeked in.

Rosario, Mike, and David were still sitting against the wall, but Emily was standing over to one side. She looked like she had slipped into shock.

Big inbred assclown, aka the drawler, was standing in front of

David, holding his gun against David's head.

This arrangement put a big crimp in my plans.

The drawler spoke to David. "I bet you look at her all day long and think about how you want a piece of that. Well now I'm going to take your piece."

"Oh really," David drawled back. He seemed to be having trouble getting the words out. "I don't think so. I don't think you have the stones."

"Oh no?" said the drawler, and he swung the gun out to the right. I stepped forward and raised the gun I'd borrowed from 9mm, but before I could do anything else, David wrapped his feet around one of the drawler's boots, and pulled. The guy lost his balance and toppled forward. I ran into the room and punched him in the neck. I'd been planning to pistol-whip him but at the last moment thought better of it. I figured I'd be permanently banished from The Chief's imaginary task force if I gave someone else a head injury.

The gun fell out of the drawler's hand as he kept falling forward onto David, until his head crashed against David's own noggin. David reached up and pushed him back. "Die, scum," he said, jabbing his fingers into the guy's eye sockets through the ridiculous pantyhose.

I laughed as David leaned back, panting. Out of my peripheral vision I sensed the others, in various postures of shock and dismay, but I felt like there was something about David that required my attention. He looked sort of gray, and he was listing to one side, like a boat that's been capsized.

Then I remembered Douglas Schenker.

I turned and sprinted out of the room and down the stairs. A moment later I was back. I kneeled next to David and propped up his head.

"Eat this," I said, slipping an aspirin under his tongue. I'd already called 911.

CHAPTER TWENTY-EIGHT

Even though she'd been up past two o'clock, Karen was awake that morning by seven, energized by her discoveries of the night before. She had coffee and dressed, then went for a walk, but she couldn't seem to calm her mind or dissipate her excess energy.

Most of all, she found herself wanting to tell Gail and Emily what she'd found out.

"Why don't you call Emily at the city offices when they open at eight?" Joe suggested. "And if you like, you can invite them to dinner again."

She knew it was a sensible suggestion, but it wasn't what she wanted.

At a few minutes after eight, she grabbed the car keys. "I'm just going to run down there," she said.

Joe looked startled, but he merely smiled and waved.

When she arrived at the Community Development office half an hour later, she was surprised to find the reception area completely empty.

"Hello?" she called down the hall. There was no response. Then she heard some muffled thumping from the meeting room above her.

She climbed the stairs to the conference room and opened the door. Gail, Emily, and another woman Karen knew to be Rosario Gardner, along with two men Karen recognized as city employees, were all present, all wearing nothing but their underwear. Another man, who was dressed and had some sort of covering over his head, was sprawled out on his stomach and seemed to be unconscious. Meanwhile, Gail and Emily appeared to be administering first aid to one of the two underwear-clad men, who was on the floor in the recovery position.

"What the hell?" Karen exclaimed.

Their eyes all turned toward her. Then Gail started to laugh. "Hey, Karen. Do we know how to party, or what?"

Just then a voice spoke behind her. "Excuse me, ma'am," it said and a hand gently but firmly brushed her aside as two paramedics and a swarm of policemen rushed into the room.

Chapter Twenty-Nine

The next day was a Friday. Patrick gave the whole Community Development Department the day off. (We'd been closed for most of the day Thursday, of course, recovering from our various physical and mental injuries.) Patrick called us all at home Thursday afternoon to let us know he'd made arrangements for a trauma counselor to be available for appointments Friday or at any time over the weekend, should we care to avail ourselves.

I thought that was sweet, but I was actually feeling pretty solid after a whole afternoon and evening with Chris, who rushed home from school as soon as I called to tell him what had happened.

When he got home I was standing at the kitchen counter, cutting my yellow, satin, polkadotted underwear into tiny squares with a pair of scissors. I'd changed into plain white cotton underwear and sweats as soon as I reached the house.

Chris set down his briefcase and watched me work for a moment. Then, "Cootified, huh?" he asked.

"Beyond repair."

He stepped over close to me and traced his finger in a pattern on my arm.

"Circle circle, dot dot, now you've got a cooties shot."

I snorted. "You're ridiculous."

"True," he said, picking up my fragments of fabric and tossing them into the garbage can under the sink. "But listen, Mike called while I was on my way home. He's worried about you.

Said one of those psychopaths had you out of sight for a while. He didn't try anything, right? Of a sexual nature? 'Cause I can run out to the jail in Milton and strangle him real quick. Wouldn't take more than an hour. I'd still be home in time to make you dinner."

"Well, he did touch my left breast, but only because I invited him to."

Chris sighed audibly. "I assume you had your reasons."

"I did. I needed him to stretch out his arm so I could break it."

"That's my Amazon." He folded me into a hug. "Seriously— are you okay?"

"A little shaky, but not too bad. Mainly I'm just burning the adrenaline off at this point."

"What do you want to do? Do you want to take a nap? Do you want a foot rub? Or maybe go for walk on the beach?"

"All tempting, especially the foot rub. But what I really feel like doing is driving over to the Funplex and hitting some balls."

So that's what we did. After an hour in the batting cages, I wasn't so wound up anymore.

On Friday morning I got up with Chris and followed him around while he got ready for work. He offered to stay home again, but I told him to go. I wanted to get things back to normal as quickly as possible.

Since I didn't have to go to work myself, I called Emily to see if she wanted to visit David, who'd been taken directly to the hospital at the end of our adventure the previous afternoon, under suspicion of a heart attack.

Em said yes, so I picked her up a little before 10 o'clock. In the hospital lobby we ran into Rosario, who had just bought a flower arrangement in the gift shop. She added our names to the card and we rode up to the second floor together.

As we exited the elevator we ran into David's wife, Carol. She looked a little harried, but otherwise composed, as she reached out to give each of us a half hug and an air kiss. "Go on down," she said. "It's a regular Gulf Breeze City convocation in there. I'm just going to run and see an inning or two of Heather's softball game, since y'all are providing so much company for David."

When we got to the room, we found it already crowded with Patrick, Mike, and The Chief. "Now it's a party," David said as we entered the room. He had the bed propped up to a sitting position and looked a little pale, but otherwise much better than when I saw him last.

"It looked like y'all were having plenty of party yesterday when I got to the conference room," The Chief said. We all laughed. Even Rosario giggled nervously. I was glad The Chief was helping us make a joke of it. By the end of the previous morning, I'd been afraid I might never see Mike, Rosario, or Emily again. They seemed likely to wander off into the sunset, rather than return to a world where coworkers had seen them in their underwear.

"So when are you blowing this clambake?" I asked David.

"The doctor says I should be able to go home by Sunday, if all goes well. It was a very mild heart attack. I don't need angioplasty or anything."

"A warning shot across his bow," The Chief said.

"He must change his life," Patrick added.

A nurse came in. "Mr. King needs his rest," she said, looking at us disapprovingly.

"It helps me to overcome the trauma of yesterday's events to have my colleagues around me," David said, batting his eyelashes as the nurse.

"Five minutes."

When she was gone, The Chief said, "So, Gail, we've been

talking it over, and we've decided to arrange a transfer for you from Mike's department to mine. It's the only solution. Clearly you're a born cop."

"Born cop? You don't see her sitting around eating donuts and writing traffic tickets, do you?" David asked. "She's more like some kind of ninja."

"Hillbilly ninja," I said.

"Seriously, Gail, thanks for everything you did for us," Mike said.

Everyone else quickly chimed in with their thanks. I could feel myself blushing.

"All in a day's work," I muttered.

Then, much to my surprise, Rosario took my hand. "Keith would have been very proud of you, honey."

I turned away so they wouldn't see a hillbilly ninja cry.

About an hour later, I'd dropped off Emily and was headed for home when I noticed a truck behind me. That wasn't so unusual. The Redneck Riviera is full of trucks. But I was feeling rather jumpy, after all the excitement of the past few days, and something about the truck rang my alarm bell.

Though it wasn't my normal route, I made a left onto College Parkway, then another left onto Duke. I stayed on Duke parallel to 98 for half a mile, then wound south through the Whisper Bay subdivision and back onto 98. The truck stayed with me the whole way.

For the first time I felt genuinely sorry I hadn't taken up Mike on his offer to arrange a concealed weapons permit. I'd be shooting out that jackass's tires right this minute.

Since that wasn't an option, I slammed on the brakes. As my F150 came to a sudden stop, I watched the truck behind me swerve onto the shoulder to avoid hitting me. I pulled over in front of him and jumped down to the road.

The man behind the wheel of the Chevy, curly haired and in his early 40s, stared in astonishment as I stormed toward him. "You want a piece of me!" I roared, pounding on the Chevy's hood. "Come and get it!"

The man look petrified. He was alone. For the first time it occurred to me that maybe he hadn't been intending to terrorize me after all.

"And if not," I said in a more normal voice, "then why the hell were you following me?"

The man rolled down his window a few inches. "I'm sorry I scared you. I know you've been through a lot during the past few days. I was just hoping we could talk for a few minutes. I'm Chip Brown."

Ten minutes later we were sitting in a deserted corner of the public library.

I settled awkwardly into a beanbag chair while Brown sat opposite me on a low upholstered loveseat.

"I'm all ears."

Brown exhaled heavily and dropped his hands to his sides. "Where to begin. It all started with the Eglin parcel, I guess. I've had my eye on that parcel for a long time. I'm friends with Ken Davis, who did the Hilton resort out there. It turned out to be a nice investment, and he made a bundle. And I had this idea that was sort of unique, for a resort that would cater to the families of enlisted men and women. I thought it would be a way of giving something back to the troops."

He seemed to be seeking my approval. I wasn't inclined to give it, at least not until I knew what was going on. But he looked at me so anxiously I found myself relenting. "I did think that was a nice idea."

"Thank you. But the old Director of Land Use at Eglin wouldn't have anything to do with it. Did you know him?

I shook my head. "I don't even know the current Director of Land Use."

"Ah. Well, Edwards was more up your alley. A conservationist." (*How*, I wondered, *did I wind up being classified as a treehugger?* In college I'd worked to appear neutral, and had distanced myself from the more political students. But sometime during the past two weeks, I'd crossed some invisible line. What Brown said was now true.) "He thought Eglin had already parceled off too much land for private development. Wetlands in particular. He didn't care whether the parcel was already surrounded by development. After the Fischer parcel was leased out for the steakhouse, he made up his mind not to approve any more lease transactions.

"But Edwards retired last year, and the new Land Use Director quickly made it clear he was *very* interested in commercial development. With the economy being how it is, even the military is feeling the pinch, and Swanson figured he could generate some revenue for the base.

"At least, that's what he told me when he contacted me about getting the resort project going again. He asked Bradford and me to come to a meeting he'd arranged about it."

"Bradford? As in, Bradford the Yellow Tree developer? Disappearing Dan Bradford?"

"Yeah. He's my cousin. He was my silent partner on this project. I figured y'all didn't know about that, since his name wasn't on any of the paperwork. We've both been involved in land development for a while, and we always said we wanted to work on a project together sometime, and we figured this was the one.

"So we went to Swanson's meeting, and McKinley Deaver was there. Swanson told us that rather than trying to do wetlands reclamation ourselves, we should use Deaver's new mitigation bank. He was going to charge us about three times the going acreage rate for land in Milton, but we were getting such a good deal on the land lease that seemed fine."

"Was it your impression that approval of your project was contingent upon you mitigating with Deaver?"

"Danny and I talked about it afterward. It definitely seemed like we were being wrapped up in a package deal. But they did it with a pretty light hand at the time. It was only later that we understood how deep we were in."

"Is that why he decided to do the disappearing act?"

"Yeah. After your friend was kidnapped, everyone got freaked out. The cops went and talked to Deaver when they found out about Belie Jenkins's mitigation bank obsession. Deaver was pissed. He didn't like the cops looking at his business—and he didn't like you and your friend sniffing around, either. He started trying to micromanage the project. He was calling Danny and me three times a day, wanting to know exactly where we were and what we were doing.

"It made us a little skittish. Especially Danny. And after Deaver told him the kidnapping was tied up with the mitigation bank . . . well, he just got really freaked. Said he didn't want to have anything to do with it. I was starting to feel the same way. I know people think developers are crooks, but everything I've been involved with was pretty straightforward. Danny, too. I know you're not a fan of Yellow Tree, but that was a case where the market collapsed before he was able to finish the project. It was nothing more complicated than that."

I nodded acknowledgment. No use arguing about it right now.

"We were starting to feel like we were in over our heads. So Danny called Swanson. He said, 'Look, some poor lady's been kidnapped over this mitigation bank situation—maybe Chip and I should just count on doing the wetlands reclamation ourselves.' There's a lot of wetlands acreage available around here, you know. We could have done it, for cheaper than what we were paying Deaver. But evidently Swanson got pretty huffy with Danny.

"Danny came to see me that night. He was a mess. He said he didn't understand what was going on, but he didn't like it. He couldn't sleep, and he kept throwing up when he tried to eat. He looked terrible. He said he was done with Eglin.

"I felt pretty much the same way. And one thing you need to know is, at this point, we hadn't signed anything. There was no contract with Eglin, there was no contract with Deaver. We were out a few thousand for the engineering drawings and a few fees. But that was it. There was no reason we shouldn't have been able to walk away at that point."

"But there was some objection?"

Brown rubbed his hand over his face. "We called Swanson the next morning and told him. He didn't say a whole lot. But about an hour later, Deaver showed up at my house. He went berserk. Threatened us, threatened our families. Said he and Swanson were giving us the chance of a lifetime to make a nice little bundle of money, and we were acting like a couple of pansies. He basically told us we had no way out.

"Danny bailed the next day. He's divorced, and his ex and their daughter are up in Chicago. He figured if he disappeared Deaver would let him go."

"Kind of left you holding the bag, huh?"

"Up until now. Once Danny was gone I figured I should just play along for a while. My son joined the Air Force in January. He's been waiting for orders, and he just found out yesterday they're shipping him out west. My ex is going back to her family in Mississippi. And I'm heading out, too. We've got some family property in New Orleans. I'm just going to get lost over there for a while."

"That sounds like a good idea." I was tired, and wasn't sure I was tracking everything Brown said. I would have to sort it all out later. But there was no question that getting out of this deal sounded like a good choice.

Then something occurred to me. "What does Australia have to do with any of this? Do you know?"

Brown looked startled. "You know about that, huh? When Deaver came over to my house that morning, in the midst of his rant, I think he told Danny and me more than he meant to. He said him and Swanson had friends in high places. They were working on making the Florida mitigation bank system the model for the whole country. That would mean people like Deaver could get consulting gigs all over the country—not to mention they could snatch up any suitable land before anyone else even knew about it."

"Karen and Emily sort of figured that. But what's that got to do with Australia?"

"I'm getting to that. Deaver said his friends in high places—we figured a U.S. Congressman, at least—were looking at the Eglin/ Park Service/mitigation bank swap as a model for getting National Park land into the hands of private developers."

"But that's illegal."

"It always has been up till now. But he said if this 100-year lease went through for our project on Eglin, they were going to use the same land swap model to start leasing out land in the national park system for things like hotels, concessions, restaurants."

"That's crazy."

"I would have thought so. But Deaver said it was an idea whose time had come. He said his 'friends in high places' thought there was still a lot of resentment in this country about the way Clinton yanked all that land into the park system right at the end of his tenure. They thought they could use the mitigation bank angle to pitch the land lease swap as environmentally friendly."

"I can see why they'd be foaming at the mouth to get a piece of that. Almost 300 million people visited national parks last year. If each of them spent just $10 while they were there, you'd be talking about a $3 billion a year industry. But I still don't know what this has to do with Australia."

"Deaver said Australia recently passed a law allowing the government to award concession and lodging franchises within its national park system to private developers. That was the model, the goal. But he said there were still too many bleeding hearts in this country for it to pass directly, so they had to do a runaround."

"I appreciate you telling me all this." I looked up and noticed one of the librarians giving us the stink eye. Gulf Breeze has one of those old-fashioned libraries, where you can still be shushed for talking. "I guess we'd better get out of here."

"You and your friends better take care of yourselves. I doubt they'll try something again as crazy as what went down at the city offices the other night—I'm guessing Deaver flew off the handle and a couple of his goons misinterpreted his orders. But you've made an enemy, for sure. Probably more than one."

We struggled out of our squishy chairs. Out in the parking lot I said, "You take care of yourself too, you hear?" and stuck my hand out.

Brown smiled as he shook my hand. "You're not going to let this go, are you?"

I smiled back. "Probably not."

Brown laughed. "Well, best of luck to you. You have a bigger pair than mine. I knew that before I even met you, and everything I've seen today only confirms it." Suddenly he looked serious. "No offense meant."

I laughed as I climbed into my truck. "None taken."

CHAPTER THIRTY

After they took him off life support, Belie lived for 11 more days. He died the same afternoon David King was released from the hospital. The Chief called Karen to let her know. The family buried him right away, without a service.

On Monday, Karen told Joe she needed to think and was going to drive over to the beach for a nice long walk. But instead, she crossed the Garcon Point Bridge and drove north until she hit Memory Park Cemetery, just off Route 90 in Milton.

She drove around until she found the grave that hadn't been re-sodded yet. A small gray stone served as a marker.

Belie Jenkins

1943–2009

A Conservationist

and A Good Son

She was contemplating this description when a man approached. He appeared to be in his early 60s, about the same age as Karen herself. He was wearing jeans, a plaid shirt, and a belt with a huge metal buckle depicting a 12-point buck. He held a Styrofoam cup in one hand. As she watched, he spit discreetly into it.

Karen felt her nervous system shift into overdrive, but she fought the impulse to run screaming back to her car.

The man joined her in front of Belie's gravestone and stood

contemplating it for a moment.

"You the lady?" he finally asked.

Karen knew what he meant. "Yeah."

The man nodded. "I'm his cousin Eddie."

"I'm sorry for your loss."

The man nodded again and spit into his cup. "I don't suppose Belie had much business snatching you up like that. He never had both oars in the water anyway, but after Korea he didn't even have one oar in no more."

"Did he ever talk to anyone about it? You know, like a therapist?"

"Naw, that's not the Jenkins way. He just hung around running errands for his mama and going off his nut about the swamp. I guess you two had that in common."

"I guess we did."

"It's probably nothin' special to you, but I ain't never seen anything like him. A few years back, our Uncle Don got up a duck hunt one weekend. We had some blinds out in the swamp, and Don wanted all the menfolk to go out together. By then, Belie didn't go on family outings so much anymore. But Uncle Don insisted all the male cousins had to go.

"Belie wound up in the same blind with me and our cousin Joey. The sun had just come up and we were just sitting around. To tell the truth, I don't care for duck hunting so much. I was hoping to maybe see some deer. All of a sudden I look across the bog and I see these tall grasses that are all sort of feathery on the top.

"I said, 'Hey, Belie, isn't that some of those sea oats you're so crazy about? You know, the ones that prevent *dune erosion*?' "

"Belie looks over and he says, 'Those ain't sea oats. You won't see sea oats up here. Water's too brackish. Those are Phragmites.' "

"Cousin Joey said, 'Phrag *what?*'

"And Belie says, 'Phragmites. The common reed. Such as sheltered the baby Moses when Jochebed hid him from the Pharoah's wrath.'

"Well, it sounded like Belie loved those Phragmites just as much as sea oats, and I told him so. I was yanking his chain, but Belie just got all thought provoked and said, 'Hard to say. Some ecologists consider Phragmites a nuisance. They invade marshes and overtake the ecosystem, crowding out other plants and even animals. Others say Phragmites marshes are valuable wetlands in and of themselves.'

"Joey said, 'Belie, cut to the chase. Are they *good* or are they *bad*?'

"And Belie said, 'Personally, I can't see how the reeds that saved the baby Moses can be anything but good.' "

Cousin Eddie spit in his cup again. "I knew it surely meant the End Times were nigh—the Jenkins family tree being invaded by a treehugger. But I have to admit, I was impressed, hearing Belie talk like that."

The man touched her lightly on her shoulder, then wandered off again. Karen watched until he was out of sight. Then she turned back to the grave and set down what she'd brought—a bundle of dried sea oats.

"So long, Belie. Looks like it was you who turned out to be the Martyr of Mitigation, after all."

ABOUT THE AUTHOR

Dawn Corrigan holds an M.F.A. in poetry from the University of Florida. Her poems, short fiction, creative nonfiction, and business writing have appeared in more than 80 print and online journals and anthologies. She was one of the founding members of the blogging collective *The Nervous Breakdown,* where she wrote from 2006 until 2009, and from 2009 until 2011 she served as associate editor of the online journal *Girls with Insurance.* Her work has been nominated for a number of best-of awards including a Pushcart, the Million Writers Awards, and Best of the Net. Since 2010, she's worked for the City of Pensacola Housing Office, administering housing assistance programs for low-income families.